C0-AZR-455

Letters to Our Children

Lesbian and Gay Adults Speak to the New Generation

Compiled and edited by

LARRY DANE BRIMNER

The Lesbian and Gay Experience

FRANKLIN WATTS

A Division of Grolier Publishing
New York London Hong Kong Sydney
Danbury, Connecticut

Acknowledgments
The author and publisher gratefully acknowledge permission from each of the
essay contributors the right to reprint their copyrighted essays.

Photographs courtesy of: C.F. Clifton: 12; Cathy McKim: 28; Ronnie Sanlo: 36;
Glenda M. Russell: 44; Richard Strickland: 50; Gary Mallon: 58; Sieglinde
Friedman: 66; Eddie Conlon: 70, 71; Bruce Becker: 76; Archbishop Mark
Shirilau: 88; Elizabeth Cramer: 108; Joan Sage: 114; Steven LaVigne: 121;
Christine Kehoe: 129.

Library of Congress Cataloging-in-Publication Data

Brimner, Larry Dane.
    Letters to our children: lesbian and gay adults speak to the new
  generation / compiled and edited by Larry Dane Brimner.
      p. cm.--(Lesbian and gay experience)
  Includes bibliographical references and index.
    Summary: Gay men and lesbians from all walks of life describe their
  personal experiences, travails, and triumphs.
    ISBN 0-531-11322-1 (lib. bdg.)   0-531-15843-8 (pbk.)
    1. Gay men--United States--Correspondence--Juvenile literature.
  2. Lesbians--United States--Correspondence--Juvenile literature.
  [1. Gay men. 2. Homosexuality.] I. Series
  HQ76.2U5B55   1997
  305.9'0664--DC20   96-36213
                                   CIP
                                   AC

Contents

Introduction

When young people observe the world around them, the images that usually greet them are those of heterosexuality. We live, after all, in a culture that is heterosexually biased, with marriage between a man and a woman its brightest beacon. These images are pervasive in our culture, though many of them are so subtle as to barely merit recognition. But they are there just the same. Walk by a bakery in the spring and you'll likely see the traditional couple—male and female—atop a wedding cake displayed in the window. Tune in to television, and a popular vitamin commercial shows a senior couple—male and female—out for a walk in the country. Without announcing it, these images convey heterosexuality.

For the most part, television programs and movies have perpetuated this heterosexual bias by focusing on traditional families. True, *The Brady Bunch* and *Leave It to Beaver* have given way to *Cybill* and *Dr. Quinn, Medicine Woman*. But the underlying heterosexuality of these programs is still there. Until very recently, the gay and lesbian characters one encountered in these media were objects of derision or pity. They were secondary characters added to give a story line a little spice or some comic relief, often at the expense of the homosexual character's self-esteem. When you're in the majority, as heterosexuals are, and the minority sits by quietly, as homosexuals did for too long, ridicule is gotten away with easily.

More recently, happy, healthy homosexuals have gained exposure and heterosexual acceptance on both the big and little screens, and make no mistake, these are positive strides. But with the plethora of "drag" movies, *To Wong Foo . . .* and *The Birdcage* to name but two, one wonders if by perpetuating the stereotype of male-homosexual-as-drag-queen, one isn't kowtowing to the old notion that heterosexuality is somehow better, even if it lacks taste and sensibility. More importantly, one also must wonder if the underlying message such films send to gay youths is that "If you want to be a happy, well-balanced homosexual, you had better step into heels and a dress." Too often, the images of homosexuality that are portrayed in the media are distorted or limited and fail to take into account the true diversity that is so common in the real world, so common in the real homosexual community.

Where are the doctors, lawyers, postal workers, teachers, cowhands, truckers, and politicians? These are your everyday homosexuals; gays and lesbians who are involved in myriad occupations but remain hidden from the mainstream eye. Where are the young lesbian families trying to raise their children and the elderly gay couples tending to each other's needs? These are the faces of homosexuality that typically go unseen.

The widespread absence of positive homosexual images is no accident. In a society that is controlled by heterosexuals, many of whom are still not at ease with their own sexuality, they seek to reinforce themselves and to manipulate future generations by erasing references to homosexuality. Many—the Jerry Falwells, James Dobsons, Patrick Buchanans, Jesse Helmses, and Ralph Reeds of the world—would just as soon erase it completely, a "symbolic annihilation" by those in power.[1] But annihilation, symbolic or otherwise, hasn't worked. Gay and lesbian youths continue to come of age in spite of a society that overwhelmingly tries "to recruit them into the heterosexual lifestyle,"

6

to paraphrase an argument often made by opponents of gay visibility. The only thing they succeed in doing is making life difficult for young gays and lesbians—or unbearable. At least 30 percent of all teenage suicides are gay related.[2]

Simply put, heterosexual society is not going to provide an example for gay and lesbian youth. It will not. It cannot.

At the same time that heterosexual society has ignored sexual-minority youth, adult gays and lesbians haven't hotfooted it to the forefront to be role models and to smooth the way for them either. Michelangelo Signorile noted that "there seems to be little genuine interest among many gay adults in how the next generation of out homosexuals really thinks about themselves, the rest of us, and the world."[3] In speaking about the adult gay community, 18-year-old Renee McGaughy commented, "I think that the adults don't take enough initiative to give positive role models to gay kids."[4] *All* kids need positive role models, not just heterosexual kids; gay and lesbian adults need to be willing to take the next queer generation under our wings. If we don't, who will show them the ropes? Who will show them how to negotiate the gay community? Who will show them how to survive in a heterosexual world?

Understandably, many gay and lesbian adults turn a blind eye to the younger generation. Some have buried their own teen anguish deep inside; they don't recall what it was like to be young and attracted to someone of the same sex on a junior-high or high-school campus where the epithet "faggot" or "dyke" is tantamount to being labeled a social untouchable. Others are fearful. They don't wish to be labeled "recruiter" or "molester," charges that conservatives often make—in spite of documented evidence that heterosexuals are more likely to prey on the young, in spite of the fact that "recruitment" is geared overwhelmingly toward heterosexuality. Yet, this fear is very real. Brian McNally expressed it this way in *The Advocate*, "Our intentions can be misrepresented. No adult wants to be falsely accused of 'molestation.' Once that 'scarlet letter' is placed on an individual, it's impossible to get it off."[5]

This isn't to say that *no* gay and lesbian adults care. Quite the contrary. Without caring, concerned adults, youth-oriented social service agencies, such as Chicago's Horizons and San Francisco's LYRIC and a handful of others, could not function as effectively as they do. But the interaction with youth at these agencies is always "clinical" in nature; adults and youth do not meet or socialize outside the confines of the agency. This restriction provides accountability for the agency, a necessity in a society that is quick to make accusations of wrongdoing.

Heterosexual youth, on the other hand, socialize with their adult counterparts at every turn. There are ball games and camping trips and dances and just plain hanging around under the hood of a car. This mentoring is part of growing up. But young gays and lesbians seldom have that same opportunity within a gay context. They typically do not accompany their adult counterparts to gay sporting events or rodeos or any of the other wholesome activities that abound. The history of taboos is too long, the fears too great. But young gays and lesbians are crying out for such mentoring, for someone to show them that they can be gay and happy and successful, and for someone to listen.

In *Letters to Our Children: Lesbian and Gay Adults Speak to the New Generation*, adults take up the challenge to mentor today's queer youth. It was compiled to give you, the next generation of out homosexuals, a chance to hear, a chance to socialize with, gay and lesbian elders. You'll hear about mistakes that were made, because we all have made them and, with luck, learned from them; perhaps our experience will save you some time, energy, and heartache. Some authors turned their attention to paths you might follow if you wish to make an impact on the social and political landscape. Every generation searches for leaders, and there's no reason why you cannot become one. Relationships? Those are discussed, too, just in case you're someone who thinks you would like to couple and nest. There is talk of gay-friendly colleges, because you need to prepare for the future, and two very different essays discuss the value of change. Finally, there's Uncle Charley. Ultimately, this book is about the Uncle Charley's we all wish we had had. Let us, the contributors to this book, be your Uncle (or Aunt) Charley.

Larry Dane Brimner
Dolores, Colorado
June 1996

A NOTE ON TERMINOLOGY

Most contributors to this book used the terms *gay* (for male, or for males and females combined) and *lesbian* (for female). In at least one instance, an author spelled out *gay*, *lesbian*, *bisexual*, *transgendered*, and *transsexual*, while another used the generic and affirmative *queer*. In all cases, the terms used are meant to be inclusive of all sexual minorities, even when space didn't permit the specific terminology.

All in the Family

It has been said that the strength of a people, the strength of a nation, lies in the strength of its families. Realizing this, intolerant individuals—especially politicians and conservative religious leaders—have picked up the "family values" banner and claim that homosexuals are antifamily. Just how they're antifamily is never explained. Homosexuals are born into families, raised by those families, and—for the most part—long to retain those family connections after self-acknowledgment of their sexual orientation. Many families, however, make this difficult.

Here are some facts. Thirty percent of teenage suicides are estimated to be by gays and lesbians. Fifty percent of gay youth experience serious depression and suicidal feelings as compared to 19 percent of heterosexual youth. Twenty-five percent of runaway teens are gay or lesbian—though many of these must be more accurately called "throwaways." Twenty-six percent of gay male teens living on the street had been forced by their parents to leave home because they were gay.[1] If the strength of a nation is measured by the strength of its families, then families need to reconsider the wholesale disposal of their gay and lesbian children. This is especially true of those who tout family values and "a return to morality." How moral is it to set children up for suicide? How moral is it to cast them into the streets?

All families—and there probably isn't one without a "funny uncle" or "spinster aunt" somewhere in its arbor—might learn about the bonds of family love from the example of Hector and Pedro Zamora. Pedro Zamora was a courageous young AIDS activist. He was seventeen when he told his father, Hector, of his HIV status and sexual orientation. Did his father cast him into the streets? No, his father embraced him and told him, "The love of a father must be unconditional." And it was from his father and his family that Pedro drew his strength to speak out about AIDS. Until his death, he kept a framed picture of his mother and father in his house. Today, Hector keeps it on his dresser. At the edge of the frame is a plastic heart with the inscription, Amame como soy.

"Love me as I am."[2]

Chapter One

A Command Performance for Uncle Charley

By John McFarland

I was eight years old the first time I heard about Uncle Charley at Aunt Kate's house in Somerville, Massachusetts. I was putting together a puzzle of the map of the world on a card table when Aunt Kate said, "Charley called last night." The room immediately went silent.

"Is he here?" my father asked.

"No," Aunt Kate answered. "He called from some barroom in New York. I could hardly hear his pitch for money over the clinking of the four thousand whiskey glasses and the screams of all the floozies."

"What did he need the money for?" Aunt Sal asked.

"He didn't say," Aunt Kate said. "Probably wanted it to throw away on another of his girlfriends."

While I tried to jam pieces of Europe together, everyone else in the room put in their two cents about Uncle Charley and covered the high points of his story for me. He was the baby of the family and knew how to get his way from the time he was two years old. He was such a talented actor and so incredibly handsome. And *then* that older woman snared him into marriage and *ruined* him. I looked up from the mess I was making with the weirdly shaped pieces of the world to see them all shaking their heads about what a waste Uncle Charley's life had turned out to be.

"But, anyway," Aunt Kate said, "I sent him twenty bucks. He made me laugh."

"If I make you laugh, Kate," my father said, "will you give me twenty bucks?"

Aunt Kate roared with laughter, slapped my father's knee and said, "Go on now, I'd be penniless if I did that, wouldn't I?"

13

A few weeks later, my friends and I were going through the trash in the alley behind the Brattle Theater in Cambridge. Because the directors of the theater had decided they were never going to stage plays again, they had tossed costumes, props, scenery, and every other kind of theatrical doodad out the back door into the alley. In the middle of all this good stuff was a big green cardboard poster advertising a production of "Hamlet."

The poster had eight glossy black-and-white photographs glued to it. Under a photograph of one of the men was Uncle Charley's name. For the first time I saw what he looked like. He was movie star handsome with thick wavy hair and a wicked smile sneaking across his lips. He was a heartbreaker, my Aunt Kate had said, and the photograph didn't make her a liar.

One afternoon about a year after I found that photograph in the trash, there was a knock on the front door. My mother opened the door and screamed, "Look at you!" It was Uncle Charley. He was very tall and thin. He was wearing a stylish tweed suit. He looked exactly like the photograph of the heartbreaker on the "Hamlet" poster. He said hello to me, shook my hand, and then sat down on the sofa. He talked a mile a minute to squeeze in every detail of what had brought him up from New York. He was in Boston for the afternoon on his way to a convention at a resort on the North Shore. He was selling women's sportswear right then, not acting. He leaned close to my mother and whispered, "Dresses, you can forget them! They're finished. The future is separates. Everything I sell now is separates."

I didn't know what he was talking about but I saw what he was: sophisticated, lively, and entertaining. My mother was totally hypnotized by him and hung on his every word as if it was coming directly from God Himself.

After he had been dazzling us for about an hour, Uncle

Charley had to leave to catch a train. For the rest of the afternoon, my mother acted as if she had taken 17 different kinds of vitamins all at once. When my father came home from work, she told him that Uncle Charley had dropped by and let her know that the future was separates.

"The future is putting the touch on your brothers and sisters," my father said. "You didn't give him any money, did you?" My mother said that the topic never came up. "That's a switch," my father said. "So the future is separates. We've learned that today, haven't we, John? Lucky us! And for free!"

What I had learned that day was that Uncle Charley was gay. I don't know how I realized that because at nine years old I wasn't exactly clear about the concept. But I knew it anyway. It wasn't just that he was handsome, exotic, and sophisticated, and knew that the future was separates. It was a deeply mysterious, instantaneous recognition on my part.

Uncle Charley's name popped up every once in a while at family gatherings when Aunt Kate had had another late-night phone call from him in New York. She would always bring up the women he was throwing away his cash on and the whole family would all click their tongues in shame. I was just a kid and yet I seemed to be the only one who knew that whatever Uncle Charley was spending his money on, it wasn't women. From time to time, I wished Uncle Charley would show up so that I could check out his moves. But at least I had seen him once and knew that there was somebody out there who probably had the answers to some of the serious questions I had later on.

For immediate answers to those questions, I had to act as my own Uncle Charley. I would mull over my questions very carefully, look in libraries for answers, and then do my best by winging it. It wasn't until college when I had a circle of other gay friends that I had people to bounce ideas off of and share information with. What I found out then, without the help of Uncle Charley, was that, although we were all gay, each of us had different experiences and different things we wanted to find out about. Sometimes we could help each other directly, but other times all we could offer was sympathy. In those discussions I learned fast that you can never underestimate the benefits of genuine sympathy. The next thing I learned was that sometimes the information you got from another person turned out to be wrong, or at least wrong for you.

For example, I had a good friend named Jimmy, whom I had met through mutual friends. Jimmy was in a committed relationship with Harry, a man who, Jimmy proudly told us, was twenty-five years older than him. Jimmy made a habit of holding forth on the joys of "marriage" and setting Harry and himself up as role models for aspiring male couples. What did we know? After all, we were the ones who spent years sneaking close looks at Harry, marveling at how well preserved he was until the day we found out he was fifteen years younger than Jimmy had said. Other key parts of the version of married bliss that we'd been sold turned out to be just as greatly exaggerated, although they too had been accepted on faith before the relationship blew apart once and for all.

There was, of course, a lesson here that Uncle Charley could have told us all right off the bat: a relationship from the inside is very different from what outsiders observe from a safe distance. And, as if to salvage some portion of the experience that had turned so sour at its end, Jimmy later turned the zest, the shared interests, and the antic fun of their time together into a marvelous children's book. On the publication of *Speedboat*, another eminent children's book author went out of his way to congratulate Jimmy by saying, "You've written the first gay children's book!" This story of two devoted male companions who sleep in the same bed and try to get along although their personalities are so incompatible is indeed a book that Uncle Charley could have wholeheartedly recommended to me.

Without helpful hints from our elders, though, we still had to rely first on discussions with our friends for what was coming next. And those discussions could be eye-openers when least expected. I remember chatting with my friend James Moore after he had returned from a Christmas holiday in Georgia. Before Christmas dinner had begun, James's eighteen-year-old nephew Danny had hugged him and said, "I'm so glad you've come home this year, Uncle James. It means a lot to me to see you, to see your example, and to know that I can be like you or not like you, but mostly myself."

"I didn't even realize Danny was gay, much less that he was watching me," James told me. "He said he looked up to me. Can you believe it?" James paused and then said, "And I thought, right, it would have been easier for *me* if my Uncle Charley had come around more instead of running off to Chicago and staying there forever."

I was amazed. "Did you have an Uncle Charley too?" I asked. Once we got over the coincidence of each of us having a gay Uncle Charley, we discussed how much we had thought about them as we were growing up and spending so many hours sneaking around the library in search of even the tiniest clue.

James and I decided then and there that what the world needed was for all the Uncle Charleys to sit down, write the book, and make the video so that the next wave of our brothers and sisters would have access to *Uncle Charley's Guide to Life As a Gay Person (Test-driven and Proven to Be True)*. Both of us knew by then that the guide *had* to feature prominently three important pieces of advice: Everyone had to value themselves first; everyone had to maintain a sense of humor; and everybody had to have the courage to live each day toward becoming the most complete person they were meant to be, though they shouldn't get so full of themselves that they wouldn't take a chance on love. But there was so much more besides those three tips that we knew our uncles could tell us if we had the chance to ask them, even now.

Chapter Two

A Letter to My Nieces

To Erin, Sarah, and Amy:

Over the past few years I have wanted to talk to you about something that is very important to me. But it seemed like the time was never right. Someone would walk in, the conversation would suddenly switch, or I would either not have the courage or the strength. I have realized now that the time will probably never be right. Perhaps this letter might be the thing to break the ice. As I begin to write, my hope is that a letter will cover everything that I want to say. But then I realize that my hope is naive at best. There is so much to say that one short or even one long letter will not serve it justice. The only way is

By David D. Clark

to have dialogues, many dialogues, where we can really talk as an uncle to his nieces, an adult to the next generation.

I have never told you I am gay. I know that somewhere, somehow, someone has told you this secret. Someone has taught you to be quiet. Your silence is apparent at Christmas, other holidays, or when we are together. None of you has ever asked who my girlfriend is or why I am not married. Over this last year as you reached the teenage years, the family has started the inevitable teasing and joking about boyfriends' names. But when the topic naturally comes to me, I notice the silence. It is deafening. The unspoken is so prevalent, and only reinforces the closet in which I have lived so many years. It is harmful to you and me. For that, I am truly sorry.

I apologize for having a secret, a mask that I have worn for years, and continue to wear in your presence. The years of secrecy are so ingrained and so hard to break. When humans get scared, they fall into what feels natural, normal, what they are used to. For years, that meant hiding in the closet and having two lives. I was constantly wondering what others would think. How could they love me when I did not love myself? How could I destroy the dreams they have created for me? How could I possibly change their minds having heard the comments that each of them, and even myself, have made? Their hatred. My hatred. I have built a very solid wall behind which I hide. I have built it so well that it is even difficult for me to tear it down. But now I am willing to open up to you, to continue crumbling my wall.

I have been coming out, telling my story—the truth—to others since 1985. At first I told only friends who were gay, then straight friends, and then some family members. I knew when I was in the fourth grade that I was gay. But in our small town, I quickly learned to be quiet, even though no one told me to be silent. I still possess two sides of my life. At work and professionally, I am very open and out. I give talks and discussions, write articles, and even teach a college class on gay issues. I am out with all of my friends and acquaintances. But my hidden life still exists with the family. Sure, Grandma, Grandpa, and your parents know that I am gay. But that is all. They do not know about my boyfriends, my vacations, my lost loves who have died of AIDS, my professional successes around gay issues, and all the other tremendous joys I have with being gay.

During my early coming out, my emotions were as changeable as the wind. One minute or situation, I was filled with rage and hatred, the next filled with love and compassion, the next I felt hollow and empty inside, and the next exhilaration. Sometimes I felt like jumping, laughing, and screaming with joy, and sometimes, I thought the tears would never stop falling. I cannot count the number of times during the rain of tears I wished I could have called someone in our family, those with whom I am supposed to be the closest, and heard a friendly voice of love on the other end.

The years of building the closet were torture: the years of dating women to cover the secret; the years of drinking to excess, and subsequently becoming an alcoholic; the years of distancing myself from the family so no one would ask; the years of working so hard, becoming a workaholic to be seen as the good little boy, the perfect man, so my sexuality would not be an issue or a problem. I got my drive not from ambition, but from running from a secret. A secret that, during points in my life, I truly hated, despised, and wished would disappear. I used women, work, alcohol, and being "too educated" to relate to anyone else to numb the secret that was putting mortar upon brick upon mortar upon brick to build my wall.

Before going into alcohol treatment, my life was on a quick downward spiral. I had an accident once while driving drunk.

Looking back, it was a desperate and purposeful cry for help. But no one heard. So I cried till it hurt, but still could not say the words. I was filled with tears, pain, and sorrow. I truly wanted to replace those emotions with love, openness, and honesty. Treatment was humbling. I was surrounded by people who were running, hiding, for a number of different reasons. I confronted my loneliness and pain. I truly realized for the first time that life was just a series of choices: to be happy or sad, to be paranoid or at peace, to live a life of secrets and shame or live a life of truth and honesty. I wanted to be whole and live my life fully.

In our family, our secrecy is prevalent, one could almost say hereditary. It is how the stoic Clarks deal with the unpleasant, or the unknown. Just like when Amy asked her mother and father if the secret phone calls at night were because of "Uncle Dave's drinking." It was a secret, but she is wiser than we wished to acknowledge. She knew something was wrong, and the innocence of the child wanted to know, wanted to help. Amy broke the secrecy by asking directly. By asking, Amy stepped across the forbidden line and started direct communication. I equate this secret, and all the other secrets, with shame. We are ashamed to tell people the truth for fear of what they might think. So we make and keep the secret, even though everyone knows the secret. Secrecy means shame. And I love you too much to continue to teach you that shame is okay, that it is normal. Now I can be honest about who I am and live life openly and fully—no easy thing to do. I did not choose to be gay, but I do choose to tell the truth. That is what my parents taught me and I, in turn, wish to teach you.

By being open, I hope we can have a greater, stronger, deeper relationship. I want us all to put down our guards and be genuine. I want us to rely on the strength that blood binds together. I do not want us to be hesitant, to always censor what we think or feel. I know that I do not act as fun loving, as happy, and as exuberant as usual when I am around you. I am guarded. I always make sure not to slip in any gay jokes, or be too flamboyant, or laugh at the "wrong" thing.

Looking back I remember fondly the times that I have watched you play soccer, softball, or give 4-H presentations. I remember the fun and laughter at family gatherings. I remember watching in awe as you grew. But I also remember being in total control of the situations, never letting the conversation get too close to the secret, never letting the conversation get too close to me. It was difficult, it was time consuming, and it was tiring. I was scared you would find out. I knew that once you knew, with the innocence of children, the secret would become known. At least with parents, I knew the secret would be kept.

I want to share fully in your lives, and share my life fully with you. I want to tell you that I am still the same man, the same uncle. Except now you know me deeper. I am still the one who loves to play catch, to play volleyball and soccer, to dance, to joke and tease. I am still the one who will forget your birthday until about a month later, but I will try to remember. But now you have more of me. For I can now be my whole self, not the censored self you have been seeing. Others will tell you that I am immoral and wicked. Please remember who and what I am to you. How can someone "immoral" have so much love for you?

When I talk to groups I destroy stereotypes. The audience often comes with the opinion that the gay issue does not affect them, that gay people are only from the cities, not the farms of Iowa. But I am living proof that gay men and lesbians are everywhere and belong to every walk of life. When I was growing up, there were no role models, no one to show me that gay people can be happy, healthy, and productive citizens. Everything I heard about being gay was that it, and secretly I, was wrong. But times have changed. My gay friends and I are strong, willful, and stubborn. We are designing and creating lives for ourselves that integrate our whole beings. We are becoming those long sought after role models for others, both gay and straight. I have found, however, that I can only change those who are willing to open not only their minds, but also their hearts.

That is one of the driving forces behind this letter. As I work with students and other gay youth, I constantly encourage them to be honest with themselves and others. But I am not, and the tug of war is raging inside and is taking its toll. How can I be a role model, asking for honesty from others, and still lead such a dual life, totally open in the professional and personal setting yet so closeted with my family. My desire to be a positive role model is in a sense "forcing my hand," making me come to terms with my duality. It feels right and good. However, it is very difficult.

Maybe you are gay as well. We should never make assumptions. It would be wonderful if you are, and it would also be just as wonderful if you are not. You are a wonder in being yourself.

I hope you never are ashamed or feel the need to hide behind a secret. I pray that you are proud of everything you are and do. People need to look at others and base opinions on the virtues of respect, honesty, hard work, love, and commitment. These are the overriding values in life that are important. We come from a long line of hardworking Iowa farm people. Iowans judge people based on their work ethic, their caring, and their loyalty to a community, not their looks, mannerisms, and quirks. That gives me hope.

Each of us has a very special gift that must be shared. My hope is that society does not dictate your every move. I hope you or a friend of yours never has to build a closet. Young people need to direct their energies in so many other areas of their lives. Energy should not be wasted in trying to keep the secrets, to numb the pain. Energy should be spent in sports, in academics, in building strong, healthy relationships with family and friends. If you ever have friends who are gay, cherish that gift with them. If they are in the closet, do not force them out, but look at yourself first. Do you make comments or jokes that reinforce their hiding? Ask yourself what risks they face and why they cannot come out. Then help build an environment so they can be honest with themselves and others, and one that exudes pride and love.

I only have one wish for each of you: to find love, happiness, and pure peace in life. I have come to realize that I would much rather be hated for who I am, than loved for who I am not. I have found that my true and genuine friends love me for the whole me, not the censored me. And that love is deep, and feels right, just, and good.

That is my story. This letter is the catalyst to and the final step of becoming a completely out person. I have learned that the human spirit is a powerful force in the face of great adversity. Always remember that a kite rises against the wind rather than with it. I have learned that human beings can be supportive, understanding, and loving creatures if they can overcome their fears and their prejudices. I may not know why I am gay, but I will continue to rejoice in that fact and celebrate the life I have been given.

I want to give you permission to talk. Ask questions of your parents and me, and demand open and honest answers. While the answers may be difficult, the result will be deeper and stronger bonds of friendship.

I love you, and always will.

Majority Rules

In a democracy, the majority rules and heterosexuals are, indeed, in the majority. But that doesn't always mean that the majority is correct, intelligent, or even morally righteous in its actions. Heterosexism is so pervasive in society that one broad assumption is made: Everybody is heterosexual. With this assumption, homophobic attitudes, or antigay sentiment, are easily justified, and with that justification, allowed to flourish.

Most homophobia is based in ignorance. But ignorance is as pervasive as is heterosexism, if recent actions in the state of Utah are any indication. There, when a handful of homosexual and heterosexual teens tried to organize a Gay/Straight Alliance at East High School in Salt Lake City, the Board of Education voted to ban **all** clubs. In support of the ban, state senator Charles Stewart said, "[I]f the only way to keep these [Gay/Straight Alliance] clubs from organizing is to ban all clubs, I vouch for that." Yet, Kelli Peterson, the seventeen-year-old who founded the club, said that its purpose was for gay kids and their straight peers to get together "to talk about career opportunities, what movies to see, and growing up gay."[1] In other words, it was to be a system of support where no other existed.

Given the antigay bias so prevalent among some members of the majority, it is little wonder that young people choose to remain closeted when they can. "But there are those who can't—or won't—hide." says 'Charley,' a high school junior. "I didn't think anything was weird at all until the fifth grade, when I started realizing that maybe something was different. When I was thirteen I figured out the label. And that's around when I started being hassled in school, people calling me pussy and fag. . . . By the ninth grade, I would be happy if I came home from a day in school and I hadn't been called faggot or cocksucker once. That's really a sad standard for what makes you happy."[2] Support systems are vital to kids, especially gay and lesbian kids; and Gay/Straight Alliance clubs can do much to balance out the harm inflicted by a heterosexist society. They also can open the minds of straight kids, even as they provide a foundation for self-acceptance and self-worth among gay kids. As the contributors note: Only with self-acceptance can real growth begin.

Chapter Three

Closets and Faggots and Dykes (Oh My!)

By Cathy McKim

Fag. Fudge Packer. Pansy. Fruit. Homo. Bum Boy. Dyke. Lezzie. Gear Box. Lesbo. Carpet Muncher. Queer. These are the verbal weapons hurled against the "abnormal, unnatural deviants" by the "normal, natural" citizenry. They're also the terms we've taken back in pride of who we are. Gay. Lesbian. Many heterosexuals hear these words and, immediately, their minds focus on two men or two women in bed. They do not think that gays and lesbians are people who have families, go to work, pay taxes, eat, drink, sleep, and die. We shop for groceries, do our laundry, and mow our lawns, but all they seem to focus on is what we do in bed. So who has the problem with sex here?

You're living in a world where heterosexuality is considered normal and homosexuality is not. The Derek Jarman–inspired T-shirt slogan says it all: Heterosexuality is not normal, just common. Straight sex is "the norm" in that it is in the majority, and our society is set up in such a way that only heterosexual relationships are legally recognized by the church and state. The vast majority of churches would never dream of performing a same-sex marriage and most would consider the suggestion blasphemous. But churches such as the Christian, nondenominational Metropolitan Community Church not only promote gay-positive attitudes and rights, but also provide the gay community with the opportunity to have their partnerships publicly recognized through holy union ceremonies. A holy union ceremony is not recognized by the state as a legal marriage; the official definition of marriage would have to be changed and governments in North America are currently unwilling to do so.

Although some corporations are allowing for same-sex spousal benefits for their medical, dental, and drug plans, gay and lesbian employees must first deal with the major hurdle of coming out at work to get those benefits. This is not an issue for heterosexuals. The U.S. military says, "Don't ask, don't tell." In 1995, the Canadian Supreme Court ruled that while it is unlawful to discriminate based on sexual orientation, gays and lesbians are not eligible to file for same-sex spousal employee pension benefits. And while there has been some headway in individual adoption cases, there is no legislation to provide gay and lesbian parents and their partners the same rights as heterosexual couples.

Lack of social acceptance disables gays and lesbians in that there is the fear and the reality of verbal and/or physical assault for simply holding a lover's hand in public, something that heterosexuals take for granted. Gay Pride Day is one of the few occasions when we can feel safe to be publicly affectionate. *Every* day is Straight Pride Day. Slowly, governments are enacting antidiscrimination and anti-hate crime legislation to include sexual orientation. The Canadian government, in the spring of 1996, added the phrase "sexual orientation" to the antidiscrimination clause of the Canadian Charter of Rights and Freedoms after heavy lobbying and pressure from advocacy groups and the public. Yet, the political right and just plain ignorant label the advocates for equality as "special interest groups" and equal rights guarantees as "special rights." Exercise your right to vote. There is nothing special about *equal* rights.

Just as there are advocates for gay and lesbian rights, inevitably there are right-wing groups and politicians who are pushing for the opposite, believing that granting "special rights" to gays and lesbians will give us free rein to fornicate in public, molest their children, and recruit their young. Know your enemy; they idolize myths while turning a blind eye toward reality. Among the most disturbing of these right-wingers are the ones who purport to be sympathetic to our "troubled lives" and offer religious and psychiatric support to enable us to become born-again heterosexuals. They say, "Love the sinner, hate the sin." The Religious Right would have us believe that we are not normal and that our sexually deviant behavior will land us straight in the fiery bowels of hell unless we repent and get straight.

Advertisers, on the whole, reinforce the stereotypes by dismissing gays and lesbians from their mainstream advertising campaigns. When included, we seldom see ourselves reflected accurately. As the mass media is a huge communication tool, the fact that gays and lesbians are largely missing from the picture leaves all of society, gay and straight alike, with few positive images of homosexuals. Popular television and film representations of gays and lesbians have ranged from the troubled, psychotic, or just plain flaming to the more recent positive images in *Four Weddings and a Funeral*, *Philadelphia*, *Friends*, *Roseanne*, and *Serving in Silence*. But the positive images are not without controversy. Only a few years ago, advertisers threatened to pull out over the Roseanne and Mariel Hemingway kiss on *Roseanne*; ABC aired it anyway. The 1995–96 season included two same-sex marriages, *Roseanne* and *Friends*, and these met with little or no outcry. With the exception of movies such as *Philadelphia* and *Four Weddings and a Funeral*, however, most gay characters are relegated to peripheral, part-time roles. *Star Trek: The Next Generation* was barraged with letters, faxes, and e-mail from gay, lesbian, and gay-supportive fans requesting the creation of a gay or lesbian character.

That didn't happen until 1995, when a heartbreaking, same-gender romance was featured in *Star Trek: Deep Space Nine*. But it did not go unchallenged. At least one local Canadian television station edited the steamy kiss scene. By the same token, *Serving in Silence* was criticized for its wimpy approach to the scenes of physical affection between Col. Margarethe Cammermeyer (played by Glenn Close) and her partner Diane (played by Judy Davis). Both *Serving in Silence* and *Star Trek: Deep Space Nine* represent crucial steps toward presenting gay lives on network television. Let the networks and producers know that you're watching and how you feel about what they're presenting.

It is true that "lesbian chic" had its time in the limelight. Whether it was a temporary fashion craze or an actual move toward positive recognition and social acceptance has yet to be seen. There is a danger in being the "flavor of the month." It melts away. But, gradually, as celebrities and public figures such as Elton John, kd lang, Melissa Etheridge, Martina Navratilova, and Svend Robinson (a Canadian political leader) come out publicly, we have a larger pool of positive role models on which to draw. And it doesn't hurt the straight population either to see that someone can be gay *and* a talented, productive member of society who is a respected member of a profession.

There will be people who will tell you that homosexuality is a choice and that you could just as easily choose to be heterosexual. Who in their right mind would choose to bring the wrath of society upon themselves by "choosing" to be something that many people fear and hate? I don't know how or why, but I really believe that people are born gay. Some people know from a very early age that they're queer while others take years to *discover* or *acknowledge* it. Some have been in long-term straight relationships, even married with kids, when they learn that they are, in fact, gay or lesbian. The *choice* comes when the decision is made to deny it and stay closeted, or to accept it and come out. Only you can know for sure if you're gay, and only you can decide what you're going to do about it. If society were more educated about and accepting of homosexuality, then coming out would not be an issue. Gays and lesbians wouldn't find themselves living a lie in unhappy heterosexual relationships or a series of dead-end, same-sex encounters.

While I strongly believe that it is important to everyone that gays and lesbians come out, I don't believe that "outing"—disclosing someone else's status as gay or lesbian—is a good idea. Coming out in situations that are physically or emotionally unsafe is not a healthy move for anyone. A person's preparedness is all. The present social climate is pretty much against coming out, and disclosing your status as gay or lesbian is a risk. But you can make it a calculated risk. You need to feel secure within yourself before you come out publicly. The less your sexuality is an issue for you, the easier it will be to disclose. Also, you need to exercise some empathy for the person you are telling. If you are ready to tell, you also need to be reasonably sure that the other person is ready to hear. Who are you telling, and why? If you're telling someone because you are concerned about maintaining a standard of honesty and integrity in your relationship, that's one thing. Telling someone in the spirit of anger or in an attempt to hurt them is another.

Coming out to family and friends presents its own unique

problems. These are people who have known you a long time and, whether they've suspected it or not, hearing that someone close to them is queer will be a new and likely startling piece of information. Parents fear the blame of society for "making you" this way, but such blame is based on myth. Siblings fear they may be, by virtue of genetics, gay too; this is another myth. Friends may fear that they will become gay by association or be labeled as such; homosexuality is no more contagious than heterosexuality. People will want to know how or why you "became" this way. When and what made you "decide" that you were going to be gay? One mother was convinced for a while that her daughter was a lesbian because she had fallen on her head when she was a child. You'll have to confront such fear and ignorance in even the most positive of scenarios. My mother asked me if being a lesbian meant that I was attracted to all women. I answered by asking her if being a heterosexual woman meant that she was attracted to all men. Once they've come to terms with the fact that someone they love is gay, it's important that our family and friends come out too. There are numerous books and groups like P-FLAG (Parents, Families and Friends of Lesbians and Gays) designed to support gays, lesbians, and their families. The more the public at large hears about us, the more likely they are to understand that there is no such thing as a single gay lifestyle. Homosexuality includes and encompasses the same variations found in heterosexuality.

It is in the best interest of everyone that gays, lesbians, and their families and friends take an active part in educating the public and speaking out against homophobia. To say that our society is biased toward heterosexuality may well be an understatement. The one thing that is certain is that the heterosexist myths about homosexuality are based in ignorance and fear. It is up to us to be out and positive. By the example of our proud lives, we show that, like heterosexuals, we are more than what we do in the privacy of our bedrooms.

Chapter Four

Celebrate Your Sexual Orientation!

By Ronni Sanlo, Ed.D.

What great and wonderful gifts you possess! Energy. Courage. Hope. A sense of immortality. You are lesbian, gay, bisexual, and questioning young people, and you are amazing to me.

Life was quite different when I was your age. I knew I was a lesbian by the time I was eleven years old, but I didn't have a name for it. You see, back then, in the 1950s, people didn't talk about being lesbian, gay, or bisexual. There were no newspaper articles, no television or movie characters, nor even conversation to give me the correct terminology with which to define myself. I only knew that I was "different" and that the difference was never discussed.

I grew up in Miami Beach. Relatives from New York and Pennsylvania would visit and invariably ask if I, the oldest grandchild, had a boyfriend yet. I wanted to say, "No! But have you seen that beautiful Annette Funicello?" I want to say that, but I didn't. I got the message very quickly, somehow, in some secretive way, that girls don't talk about other girls "like that." So I always made sure I had a boyfriend—some sweet, geeky guy ready to dutifully appear if he was needed. Heck, if he didn't appear, I would beat him up!

With no words and with no role models, I thought I was certainly the only person who felt "this way." I thought I was really sick, that if I ever told anyone, they'd lock me up and throw away the key. In fact, because of this worry, I made myself really sick. I developed ulcerative colitis, and I knew if I could just talk with someone about my feelings the internal stress I felt would go away. But there was no one I trusted enough to share such dreaded thoughts with, and I remained inside my secret self, loving my girlfriends in a private, isolated part of my heart, while openly dating most of the boys on my block at one time or other. When my father actually referred to me as "boy crazy," I realized how good an actress I could be if I put my mind to it. This was what survival was all about for me. Throughout those years, from the age of eleven to the age of thirty-one when I finally came out, I referred to myself in the third person as "that damned queer." Those twenty years were hell.

I will share some mistakes I made while on this journey to the place of celebration, where I now reside. Big Mistake Number One was not telling my parents how I felt when I was an adolescent. I am certainly not suggesting that you tell your folks; I wouldn't tell mine when I was your age. I am saying, however, that my parents were and are very good people who love all their children mightily, then and now. There is no way my parents would have disowned me, thrown me out, or in any way treated me disrespectfully. They may have been absolutely shocked; they may have been horrified. They may have taken me to a psychologist or to our rabbi. But they would not have removed me from the family, which was my absolute fear. In fact, when I decided to tell them about my sexual orientation, I did so with no hesitation, with no fear of a negative reaction. I should have told them when I was young because I would have lived my life differently and honestly, instead of amidst a pack of lies that I began to believe myself. And I wouldn't have spent twenty years silently hating myself.

When I was twenty-four my grandfather said to me, "You're almost twenty-five and not married. Are you funny or something?" In horror, I thought, Oh my God, he knows! He can look at me and tell. I had spent every waking moment from the day of realization, when I was eleven, trying to pretend to be just like everyone else. I had not told a soul about how I felt—not my sisters or brother, not my friends, not the girls with whom I had fallen in and out of love. No one. So how did this old man know? I did the only thing I could think of to veer his attention elsewhere: I got married! And then, almost immediately, I became pregnant. Now there would be no way that anyone could mistake me for being "funny or something."

My daughter was five and my son was two when I realized that I could no longer keep my thoughts and feelings hidden. I was married to a man with whom I had been close friends in college. Our marriage was nice, nothing spectacular, nothing to celebrate particularly, but not bad. My husband was an only child of parents who literally owned their own church because the believed Southern Baptists were too liberal. His parents interfered terribly in our marriage and in our lives. They were wealthy people in the habit of controlling others, including their son. We didn't get along very well, especially after the children were born.

By the time we had been married for about six years, the feelings that I had so successfully buried about my sexual orientation began to surface. There was no one to whom I was attracted, and I knew no lesbian or gay people, but by now, at age thirty, I figured out that I wasn't the only one—a revelation to say the least. Through my part time job at a fashionable department store, I met two young gay men, Richard and Tony, who didn't realize that I was coming out, but thought that I was just a good ally. They gave me a copy of *Rubyfruit Jungle* by Rita Mae Brown, and I devoured it![1] Read it if you haven't yet. It's fun and funny. In fact, Tony, who the owned the book, inadvertently helped me "out."

Tony was nineteen, flamboyant and proud of it. He enjoyed dating men who were older, much older. He was particularly fond of one man whom he wanted me to meet, so I stayed late after work one day for this event. I was excited to finally be meeting someone besides a couple of adorable, very young, Camay men. Well, his gentleman friend and I were introduced, and we nearly died of shock, Tony's friend more than I. He was my physician! He and his wife were good friends of my fundamentalist in-laws. He was an elected official in the town in which we lived. Wow! While he nearly died of embarrassment, I was ecstatic that I finally had someone to talk to. Two entirely different paradigms, but we connected and nobody had a heart attack.

To make a long story short, I filed for divorce. It was 1979 in central Florida. I felt that the divorce was entirely my fault, taking the negative perspective, so to remove any sense of guilt from my husband, I told him why I was leaving. That was Big Mistake Number Two. By telling him my sexual orientation, I lost custody of my two young children. In losing my children, I suddenly realized how powerful this thing called lesbianism must be.

I came out angry! I was furious that society kept me closeted for a third of my life, then took away my babies. I was one pissed-off dyke, and there was nothing left to lose. I quickly became immersed in politics, becoming the executive director and lobbyist of the Florida Lesbian and Gay Civil Rights Task Force in 1981. For several years I fought the hard, emotional battle of trying to break down doors, trying to change people's minds, trying to create safe places for kids in schools. My anger made me ineffective, volatile, and vulnerable. I was always on the defensive. People simply are not effective leaders when they're angry twenty-four hours a day. I was so busy fighting for lesbian and gay rights that I didn't have time to *be* a lesbian. I had no time to develop meaningful relationships, just short-lived connections.

I remember dating one woman during that time who, in exasperation with my political activity, said, "If you go to one more meeting, I won't be here when you get back." As I walked out the door to go to that meeting, I thought, I'm sure going to miss her. I had no energy to share my life, to develop intimate relationships, or to care what others thought. Like a mule with blinders, I just forged ahead, trying to make change for the better, I would say to myself and others. I collapsed in 1983 from sheer exhaustion.

As I tried to regroup and find myself within the fuzzy haze of whom I thought I was, I was nothing but a walking ball of anger. Sure, I made changes in people's lives; I had lots of feedback to that effect. But my own life was as pained as it had always been, and I couldn't figure it out. For several years I floundered, trying to find myself, being afraid to really discover myself, and staying an arm's length away from any emotional mirror. Then a woman entered my life, a straight woman about fifteen years older than me. With a gentleness I had never known and with a confidence in me that I certainly didn't have in myself, she guided me to my own heart.

During an intense personal-growth weekend to which this woman sent me, I met the anger that I harbored so tightly and discovered my reasons for hanging on to it. I began to take the emotional risks, and baby steps, to let go of the anger that had been my propulsion since I had come out twelve years earlier. The anger began to abate, and I was learning to love myself as I was, for the first time in my life—no lies, no facade, just me. The P-FLAG (Parents, Families, and Friends of Lesbians and Gays) motto, "We love our gay children just the way they are," became a personal mantra for me. I love myself just the way I am.

I began to enjoy being a lesbian, to celebrate this incredible gift, to believe that my sexual orientation is one of God's most precious gifts to me. As I opened myself to love and forgiveness—especially towards myself—I became open to receive love as well. My partner, Kathy, entered my life at that time, bringing a bounty of joy I had never known.

I began to reevaluate my leadership potential, to understand how powerful it is to lead with love and not with anger. I began to learn how individuals and organizations grow and develop, all within that silly context of love. Today, I am the director of the oldest, largest college organization that provides services to lesbian, gay, and bisexual students—the Lesbian Gay Bisexual Programs Office at the University of Michigan. I teach what I've learned—that we are glorious people and we will teach people how to treat us.

The students at the University of Michigan are learning that they, too, must lead with love, even during the times when they want to punch out some frat boy or local bigot. Lead with love. This is my message to you, the next generation of lesbians, gays, and bisexuals. We are not victims any longer, and we must not allow others to treat us as such. The students here are valued and valuable members of the university community and deserve to receive the excellent education for which they came to this institution.

And so, dear young people, as hard as it may be at times, look in your mirror and love that person looking back at you. If you are unfamiliar with lesbian, gay, and bisexual history, read some books and find out who our heroes and forebears are. We have a proud heritage and a special mission. We are the epitome of multiculturalism, crossing all boundaries of race, religion, ethnicity, ability, age, and socioeconomics. And we're pretty terrific!

My own two children? Well, we had a tough time, and it's

still not easy. For several years we were estranged. They didn't want to see me or spend time with me because of the fearful and hateful things they were told about me. But recently my daughter returned to my life and invited me to be present for the birth of my first grandchild. I was able to watch my granddaughter take her first breath in this world. My son is still very distanced from me, and yet I suspect that we have far more in common than he is aware. I trust that the angels will continue to watch over my children and that they will return to my life at exactly the right time.

You, too, are my children, of course. I have dedicated my life to paving a road out of this rocky path so that your journey will be smoother and safer than mine. Unfortunately, you will need to keep working on it for the generation of lesbian, gay, and bisexual kids following you. This work is hard, the risks are great, and at times it's awfully lonely. But the rewards, the thank-yous, the hugs, the changes in policy, the changes in laws are worth it all.

You are lesbian, gay, and bisexual young people, and you are glorious! I am very proud of you, and I am proud to be a lesbian, a mother and grandmother, and a freedom fighter of sorts. I am especially proud of the courageous young people with whom I work at the University of Michigan. I invite you to join us. In the meantime, love yourself as deeply as I love you.

43

Dear Young Gays, Lesbians, and Bisexuals

By Glenda M. Russell, Ph.D.

With some reluctance, I write to you. It is not that I don't want to share my perspective with you. In fact, I want very much to do that. It's just that writing things down often implies that they are done or complete in some way. But that is not true. We are never done with the business of growing and learning and changing, as queer people or as people in general. I would worry if I re-read this letter in five years and found that my thinking was still the same. That would mean that I had stopped learning somewhere along the way, and that would be as bad as anything I can imagine.

So I guess that's the first thing I have to say about my current perspective: It is better to grow and to change in our consciousness as lesbians, bisexuals, and gays than to be stagnant. That is true even if growing and changing involve mistakes and pain, and they often do involve one, or the other, or both. They also involve being alive and expanding.

Another part of my perspective has to do with the need to keep a balanced view of the external and the internal, where homophobia and heterosexism are concerned. Homophobia has been described as an irrational fear of queer people. Heterosexism, on the other hand, goes another step; it refers to a pervasive and deeply ingrained cultural belief that being heterosexual is superior to being gay, bisexual, or lesbian. That belief, in turn, is reflected in all sorts of social institutions. It is reflected, for example, in the institution of marriage and its exclusive availability to heterosexuals. It is reflected in laws prohibiting same-sex behavior. Homophobia and heterosexism are all over the place. If you look at them carefully, it can be a little overwhelming. Nonetheless, it is crucial that we see and acknowledge that heterosexism and homophobia exist. If we don't see them for what they are, our understanding of what is going on in the world can be very distorted. If I deny the presence of homophobia and heterosexism, I am more likely to blame myself or other gay people when I encounter homophobia and heterosexism in the world.

As an example, in 1992, the voters of Colorado, where I live, passed Amendment 2, a state constitutional amendment that basically made it legal to discriminate against gays, lesbians, and bisexuals. Understandably, lots of queer folks were very upset and hurt by this vote. People naturally need and look for explanations for big, painful events such as this. There were probably lots of factors that helped Amendment 2 to pass, but the most important was the presence of homophobia and heterosexism. But those Colorado gays, lesbians, and bisexuals who denied the presence of homophobia and heterosexism looked elsewhere for explanations of why Amendment 2 passed. Sometimes they blamed themselves, thinking they should have done more work in the campaign to defeat the amendment. Sometimes they blamed other queers, including those who worked in the campaign to defeat Amendment 2. While it's very likely that each lesbian, bisexual, or gay person could have done more to defeat Amendment 2, it's also true that mistakes were made in the campaign, as in any campaign. Nevertheless, the bottom line is that Amendment 2 passed because of homophobia and heterosexism, not because of anything that a single gay person, or gays in general, did or didn't do. If we don't take homophobia and heterosexism into account, our view is skewed. At that point, we forget what the real problem is; we can't figure out where our own pain is coming from. It is essential that we keep an eye on homophobia/heterosexism in the world.

That, however, is only half the story. I also said we need to keep an eye on homophobia and heterosexism within ourselves. No one is born with homophobic/heterosexist beliefs and feelings—no one.

We pick up those homophobic/heterosexist beliefs and feelings as we go through life. We do it virtually without knowing it. A friend of mine said it's as if we're sponges. Homophobia and heterosexism are in the air and we just soak them in. That's true of everyone, no matter what sexual orientation.

Those of us who are gay, lesbian, or bisexual have to pay attention to those homophobic/heterosexist beliefs and feelings that we have taken in or internalized. Those beliefs and feelings are there. Sometimes you can notice them in your reactions to yourself—a sense of not feeling okay about yourself, of wishing you weren't queer. Sometimes you may notice them in your reactions to other queer people—judging them especially harshly, seeing them as a group not as individuals, or wanting to distance yourself from them. Every gay, lesbian, or bisexual person I know—including myself—has had these feelings. Having them is normal.

But it's important to do something about the homophobic/heterosexist attitudes that we've taken inside us. First, don't ignore them. They won't go away; they might go underground but they won't go away. Work with them. Talk about them with other queer people who are strong enough to deal with such feelings without blame. In general, it is really helpful to be around other queer folks. There is no better way to learn the truth about who we are than to be with other gay people. If you're lucky, there is a youth group at a queer community center where you can talk about your feelings.

Learn as much as you can about queer history and culture,

too. All of this will take effort on your part. One aspect of institutionalized heterosexism is the invisibility of gay culture and history as well as of other gay, lesbian, and bisexual people. They may be difficult to find but it's important to look and to find them. Being familiar with our history and culture, our music and our coming-out stories, our political work—these are tools for undoing the homophobia/heterosexism that we've internalized. They are the tools of our strength and of our liberation.

One reason it is so important to pursue these tools is because we have to define ourselves. We cannot afford to let society define us. Their definitions are riddled with myths and stereotypes, with half-truths and lies. It is equally important that we not define ourselves in reaction to them. There is much more to being bisexual, gay, or lesbian than *not* being heterosexual. While it is, as I said earlier, important that we acknowledge homophobia and heterosexism in the world, it is also important that we not pay too much attention to people who are particularly homophobic and heterosexist. To do so is to rely on them too much for our definitions of ourselves. Our self-definitions must be rooted in who we are, not in who doesn't like us or who would do us harm.

It's a fine balance, looking on the inside and on the outside. But it's a necessary balance. One of the most obvious arenas where we see the need for this balance is in coming out. There are lots of good reasons to come out. However, sometimes there are reasons to *not* come out. For example, coming out may involve losing such things as personal safety or a job or money for your education. Those are, for some people, very real external risks. On the other hand, coming out sometimes involves internal risks: our sense of ourselves as queer people can't tolerate the questions or the possibility of rejection. Any time a person is seriously looking at the question of coming out, then you'd better be looking outside and inside. In a given situation, external homophobia/heterosexism might be more prominent. In another, internalized homophobia/heterosexism might be the bigger issue. Usually, though, both are in play somewhere and both need to be examined and understood.

Regarding life in general, whenever I find myself focusing too much on the external or too much on the internal, I remind myself to look at both. It's the best way I know to keep myself feeling safe from the outside in as well as from the inside out. It's a lot of work sometimes, but it's worth it. The rewards go far beyond mere safety. Something often happens to those of us who struggle with identity, who don't take it for granted. We don't skate through life easily, and we learn far more than we would otherwise. We learn about ourselves at a depth that eludes those who "take" whatever identity is given to them. We are stretched and we are stronger. We're frequently more interesting and more creative than we would otherwise be. I think we also have the capacity for greater compassion. It's a paradox: the more we work with our own differences and uniqueness, the more we find we have in common with others.

Chapter Six

Finding My Voice

By Richard Strickland

I could tell you many things as you grow into being the person that you are. Fundamentally, I would urge you to be true to yourself, no matter the perceived cost. Life inside the closet carries a heavy price in terms of loneliness and self-doubt, while the most fabulous company awaits you outside. Trust in yourself, in the feelings of your heart. I've repeated this like a mantra in times of my own insecurity. No one is going to make you strong. It is an exercise each of us must do for ourselves. But pathfinders and trailblazers among us enlighten our progress and offer support for flagging spirits. Reach out when you need to. I assure you someone will be there to help, support, guide, and nurture.

I spent too many years of my life imagining that I was a person other than myself, unable to accept the idea that I am gay. For a long time, I didn't even understand what it meant to be gay. I grew up in a time and a town tucked into the foothills of southern Virginia where there was no obvious hint of a gay community and no evidence of a gay man or lesbian. The transgendered people existed only in some vague notion of perversions thought to be common among the French!

Without any role models, my confused and confusing adolescence led me into greater doubt. What were those feelings I had? Why was I attracted to the Richard Gere look-alike on the football team? Why did the girls I took out on dates deride me for being too gentlemanly? I hoped and prayed that I was merely experiencing some delayed hormonal release and that some day I would experience an endocrine flush and be transformed into the raunchy stud that all high-school guys seemed to aspire to be.

Surprise! It never happened that way. As the years passed, my feelings for men grew clearer to me, though no less unsettling. Who could I talk to about this? Who could I trust? One of my problems was that I didn't trust myself, didn't love myself enough to embrace the feelings I held and live my life accordingly. Society had tacitly told me I shouldn't. I began to learn more about other gay people when I moved to the great metropolis of Cleveland. And still, I was aware of the sense that gay people lived life on the fringe, somewhere I didn't see myself. While it became easier to spot gay people, the ones that stood out were often stereotypical characters with whom I could not identify. I knew what kind of gay person I was not, but I still didn't know what kind of gay person I might be. This confusion reigned for years.

I began to grow confident enough to test my own boundaries after moving to New York City for graduate school. But then, disturbing rumors began to spread of a disease attacking the gay community, the first reports of what was to become the AIDS epidemic. Rattled by the horrors of the news, I thought it best to withdraw into my closet again, denying myself to avoid sickness and death.

But the closet is a kind of death, too. It's stuffy and dark. Mold grows there. And the spirit suffocates.

I made do in that cramped space for many more years, content to hide behind my wall of books and computer screens while I worked on my Ph.D. Everyone was willing to believe that that was such a demanding endeavor that I couldn't possibly have time for social relations, allaying their fears that I might have some other "problem" hampering my ability to woo and wed (a woman, of course). And indeed, getting to the end of the Ph.D. was demanding, time consuming, and spirit crushing. By the end, I was wrung dry, mentally and emotionally. I stood on the brink of my own future, armed with the tools to shape that for myself and claim it as my own.

And then it began to dawn on me. Just as I was about to begin shaping my professional career, I was also responsible for shaping my own emotional, sexual, and spiritual path. No one does that for you. Once you realize that, you see there really are no rules, either. Options open up. The initiative is yours. That's when living really begins!

I began to take jobs and move around the world in the course of my work. I began to see the variety of peoples on this earth and appreciate the vast array of human experiences. I began to trust myself to define my place in this world and to include my true feelings in the way I saw my life and lived it. Perhaps it helped that my work took me repeatedly to new locations where I would spend extended periods, learning about the people and their ways, and learning how to present myself and insert myself into local life. I began to value all my feelings and see myself as a worthy and integrated person. I was then able to begin to see the rich complexity of each person I encountered, and to cherish the uniqueness of each.

In this way, people became more than merely gendered sex objects to me. I began to understand why I can be attracted to men as well as to women, on many different levels. I don't have all the answers yet, and surely never will. But I have learned that I gain far more from taking a risk, seeking to connect with others, engaging in the honest exchange of emotion. Life is meant to be full of hugs and kisses, and it matters little from whom we get those or to whom we give them. Sharing them is the most important thing.

I have slowly begun to find my voice as a gay man. I will soon be thirty-eight years old. I am surprised to learn more and more men come to understand and accept themselves as gay later in life (later being a relative term, of course). It has taken me too many years, and yet perhaps I have an insight on my own life that I could not have had before. While I have been fully aware of being gay for a long time (and being somehow "different" for most of my life), it is only in the last five to ten years that I have consciously sought to accept myself and allow others to know that I am gay. The more I do that, the stronger I grow. I find strength in knowing my true self and in the solidarity I experience with other gay and lesbian people.

Perhaps no experience has been more revealing to me than my encounter two years ago with a man who became my special friend, someone with whom I shared an emotional and spiritual bond that neither of us could explain. It was only to be experienced and cherished. In a series of coincidences defying explanation, we met in a distant city where I was working temporarily. The bitterest winter on the Canadian plains fostered exchanges between strangers sheltering from the cold, people who might otherwise never address one another. In a bookstore, we met. A world of words, a place where I was comfortable as an academic and he was a pro as a poet and writer. Finally, I had found one of those gay people that I might be like after all. Confidence of ourselves led to confidence in each other. My heart blossomed despite the winter winds, and I allowed myself to trust my heartfelt feelings. I could feel myself growing emotionally each day. More amazingly, poems seemed to spring to my mind from nowhere. I found a voice to express all the feelings that I had pondered, the confusion that had ruled so much of my past, and the joy that I felt at being released from my self-imposed constraints. I also found a listener who could absorb the full measure of my words. The experience of personal growth and the increasing sense of self-worth were sensations I had longed for all my life. And they seemed to sweep over me with no effort at all.

Although we have since grown apart from each other in terms of romance, a spiritual connection with one another remains, despite the hundreds of miles between us. It seems absurd to me that heterosexuals dictate I could not or should not have loved this person because he is a man. Our lives are richer for the love we shared, and I believe that I am thus able to make the lives of those I encounter from day to day richer, too.

Giving and sharing love throughout life are elements of primary importance, defining the reason for living. Learn to trust your feelings of love: learn to know your true self. Strive to be true to who you are and you will be rewarded by the spiritual and emotional richness of others. Being gay in a straight world can be scary, I know. But you are not alone. Not ever. We are all around you. And knowing who you are deep inside is the beginning of the greatest adventure you can live.

May you grow old and prosper, secure in the knowledge of who you are and free to love the people you choose. We are all trailblazers if we choose to be.

Closets and Other Dark Places

In *Being Different: Lambda Youths Speak Out,* I wrote that:

> "The closet" became a safe place to store the gay aspect of one's identity. But harboring secrets is injurious to one's emotional well-being and allows false stereotypes to persist. Members of the younger generation have realized that beliefs many heterosexuals hold of lesbians and gays don't describe them.[1]

And so, many young people have begun to acknowledge their sexual orientation, and to embrace it publicly.

Only by standing up and speaking out can false impressions be replaced with truth. Standing up, however, takes courage and involves risk. Young people who step out of the closet can "face extreme physical and verbal abuse, rejection and isolation from family and peers."[2] Youths who take that step usually don't receive the adulation they deserve; it is a far braver act than anything their heterosexual peers will likely ever attempt, and it is an act that can be a guidepost for gay youths still inside the closet.

Stepping out of the closet and being true to yourself can be like a first breath of fresh air, as the contributors of this book report. But no youth should attempt it until there is a safety net in place. Try to gauge the reactions of friends and parents; and if there's even a remote chance that your well-being might be compromised, put off coming out until you are less dependent and more independent.

Chapter Seven

Coming Out at 35,000 Feet

By Gary Mallon, D.S.W.

"You are as queer as a three-dollar bill."

That's what my uncle told me when I was five years old and yearned to play with a Barbie doll instead of a G.I. Joe. I didn't want that short fuzzy-haired, Army-man doll. I wanted Barbie. She had long hair; she was beautiful.

I knew that I was different even then. I knew also that this was something that I was not supposed to talk about or to express in any way. My uncle and other people in my family made sure of that: "Be like all of the other boys." "Learn to play sports." "Stop trying to hang around with the adults." "Stop playing with the girls." "Toughen up, boys don't cry." And the most dreaded of all: "Stop being such a sissy!" These were the messages that I received from my own family, and they were loud and clear—don't be who you are!

As a young child, I was socialized to hide my gay identity. I hid in the world of books and in nature. Unlike most other boys, I loved reading, I loved plants, and I loved to learn about animals. I not only belonged to the Book of the Month Club, but also to the Bush of the Month Club (you got a different flowering plant every month). My family mercilessly teased me about that, but I didn't care if they thought I was strange; it was my only salvation. I furtively read books, the very few that existed, to see if there were other people who were like me. (I may have been the only eight-year-old to have checked out Kinsey's study on sexuality from the library.)

In school, I knew that some of the teachers were like me. I thought Mr. Maylon was, but I wasn't sure, and if he was he was hiding too! The only other boys who were like me were so tormented by other kids that there was no way I was going to be friends with them. They couldn't hide. I could, and I did. I'm not proud of that, but it was a survival mechanism for me.

I thought that I could never talk to anyone about being different, so I set out to become perfect. I became perfect to hide the part of me that I knew was not. I figured that if I was perfect, then if people ever found out what I really was, they would then say, "Oh, he's queer, but he's so smart," or "He's so helpful," or whatever it was that they would have to say when they found out. And I knew somehow, someday, that they would eventually find out who I really was. I dreaded that inevitability. I thought that when that day came, it would be all over, that I would be finished. I could not have been more wrong. No one ever told me that when that day came, it would be just the beginning of a real life for me.

Paul Monette, a great writer, one of "our tribe," as he would have said, wrote a wonderful book called *Becoming a Man: Half a Life Story*. In it he said, "I can't conceive of the hidden life anymore, I don't think of it as a life. When you finally come out, there's a pain that stops, and you know it will never hurt like that again, no matter how much you lose or how bad you die."[1]

It took me a long time to come out, to stop hiding; it's a process, not a one-time event and for me, it was a very long process. I hid for almost thirty years! But once I was strong or brave or ready enough to come out—I frequently say that after waiting so long I did not come out, I *crashed* out—I found that it was the most liberating and freeing experience of my life. I think that ultimately people come out when they get tired of hiding or when hiding just doesn't work for them any longer.

I thought that I was very good at hiding. What I didn't know at the time was that it distorted everything about who I was. I thought, however, that it was a very effective mechanism. I hid by doing what social workers call overcompensating. I immersed myself in books, in school, then in the Catholic Youth Organization, and later in my work. I never had time for dating. I was too busy. When my straight peers were dating in high school, I was president of the Catholic Youth Organization for the Archdiocese of New York. I was running meetings, planning conventions, running workshops, and having dinner with the Cardinal. Cardinal Cooke, who was the Archbishop of New York, was a very nice man, a very holy man. I often thought that he was one of our tribe, too. In fact, many of the people who worked in the Church seemed to be like me, so in many ways I felt very safe hiding there. After the CYO, I immersed myself in college and in my job.

I went to Dominican College in Blauvelt, New York. I studied social work and, while I went to school full-time, I got a job as a child-care worker at St. Dominic's Home working with children who were abandoned, abused, and neglected. I loved my job; I loved helping people; I still do. I didn't just work hard, I completely immersed myself in my job. These were all very effective ways of hiding an essential part of who I was.

When I graduated college, I went to work for the CYO, where I ran a wonderful youth program called Grace House in Manhattan. That's when I was first forced to deal with my gay identity.

At Grace House, I was very isolated from the people who had been my friends. I spent a great deal of time alone. Being by yourself can force you to deal with some powerful feelings. Grace House was a retreat house, a place where young people came to get in touch with who they were and with the spiritual aspects of themselves. Some of the young people who came there were openly gay. I remember admiring their courage in being out. I remember thinking, Here I am supposed to be helping them to get to know who they are and I don't even know myself. But I still was not able to come out. I was still too scared and I continued hiding.

In 1980, I went to Ireland with my sister, my father, and my mother. I returned to New York after my trip feeling very depressed and alone. Inside I was struggling to come to terms with who I was, but it was too terrifying for me to deal with. I decided that if I got married, it would all be fixed. Later that year, I met a woman I had known previously. She was an artist, a free spirit. I married her. Two weeks later, I realized that getting married was a big mistake. It was dishonest and it was unfair to my wife. It took me six months to have "the big talk." When I finally told my wife that I was attracted to men, she was understandably upset and made me promise to be faithful to her. I tried. Actually, I tried for about five years, but I couldn't do it. It wasn't fair to me, and it wasn't fair to her either.

The catalyst for coming out happened on my wife's thirtieth birthday, as we took a weekend trip to New Orleans. It was an icy, cold, January day. At the airport, before take off, I noticed a very handsome man and I thought to myself: Cute. The flight was delayed because of the icy weather and when we finally got on the plane, you could feel the tension of the other passengers because they had to keep de-icing the plane. After several de-icings, the plane took flight and when I turned to look around, the man I had noticed earlier was sitting about three rows back. When I looked back again, he winked at me. I didn't need any de-icer. I melted right there in seat J-15.

My first thought was: Too bad she's with me! My second thought was: You are a crazy man. Here you are married to this woman for over six years and you wish that she would disappear so that you could have a fling with a man who winked at you. You have to do something about this! And I did. At that moment, I was finally ready to stop hiding. I decided right there in that plane that it was time to deal with who I was. I had spent my whole life as a social worker helping others to deal with who they were, and I had spent my whole life hiding from who I was.

While in New Orleans, I slipped away from my wife and explored the gay bars. I met the man who had winked at me—his name was Mike. He was very nice. We hung out together, but nothing physical happened between us. We just talked, but I knew that I had changed. When we returned to New York, I said to my wife, "We have to talk. Our arrangement of my trying not to like guys is not working any more and I have to do something about it." My wife was upset, but tried to be supportive. It was hard for her, but I was determined not to live my life as I had. I knew that in the end such an arrangement was not fair to her either. We agreed that I would explore this part of my life, and I did.

I went out first to gay clubs with my lesbian friends, but they took me to lesbian bars. I was grateful, but I didn't find what I needed there. Soon I ventured out into gay bars by myself. I thought that I would find people like me there. I didn't realize at the time that there was another whole gay and lesbian community that was not part of the bar scene, but, like so many others before me, that's where I started. I was scared to death, I drank too much, I even resumed smoking cigarettes to calm my nerves. Scary as it was, and even though I saw some things that made me think that maybe this was not for me, I realized that I was a gay man and whatever that meant, whatever it took for me to deal with that part of my life, even if it meant I lost friends or got fired from my job, I was ready for the first time in my life to live openly and honestly. I was ready because I felt that nothing could be worse than all those years that I had spent hiding. No pain that could come my way would match all the pain that I had been through from hiding who I was. Nothing is harder than not being yourself.

Today, I'm glad to be an openly gay person. I am certain that I have made it all sound so easy, so clean, and it is not my intention to be dishonest. It was painful and messy, and while I am proud of who I am, I am not proud of some of the things that I have done on my journey to be me. Today, however, I am completely out—at work, to my friends, and to my family. My first gay relationship was with a sweet guy named Rafael. We were lovers for three years, and we shared a home for five years. Initially, we had a very nice life together, but over time our lives and our relationship changed and we separated. When Rafael was diagnosed with AIDS, I took care of him for a year. It was very hard, probably the hardest thing I have ever done. I found the stress of living day in and day out with someone who had AIDS to be very draining. After he was well enough, we decided that he should move into his own apartment. I am still a part of his support system, which is much easier than living with him every day.

Now, I have a wonderful relationship with a man who is supportive, loving, and special. We have a beautiful home in Queens, New York, that we share with our two children (he has two beautiful children who are a very important part of our lives), sometimes with my foster daughter, Leslie, who is twenty-eight years old, and with our two dogs and one cat. I have a masters degree in social work and a doctorate in social welfare. I'm an assistant professor at Columbia University School of Social Work, where I teach child welfare policy, social work practice, and a course that I designed called Social Work Practice with Gay and Lesbian Clients. I still work with kids as the associate executive director of an agency called Green Chimneys Children's Services where I run a group home for gay and bisexual kids called the Gramercy Residence.

I'm really delighted to be able to share my story with young people. I wish that I had had some adults who were able to share their stories with me when I was younger. If they had, maybe I would not have had to spend half a lifetime hiding. Hopefully, you have the support in your life from straight, gay, and lesbian people who care so that you will not have to hide, and so you will be free to be who you are. Good luck!

That Old *Difference* and *Belonging* Thing

By Sieglinde Friedman

From the time I was very young, I had always felt different from my peers. It wasn't that I couldn't do what they did or experience my school activities or friendships similarly; rather, I sensed a disparity between my outlook and feelings and those they expressed. In the end, however, what I was battling were feelings of *being different* and of *not belonging*. This puzzle took some years and misery to unravel and solve.

Growing up in the late 1960s, in an atmosphere of sexual freedom was an exciting and tantalizing time. It was all about self-expression, individuality, and testing the boundaries of cultural norms. I was sixteen years old and ready for sexual adventure on one hand, yet on the other I was uncertain; basically I was bewildered because, try as I might, I really wasn't very interested in boys (I'd always had crushes on female teachers or other women) and somehow that made me unwilling to behave in ways that attracted boys except as friends. And on top of that, my teens left me (not untypically, apparently) emotionally unsure about nearly everything and overly sensitive, especially in matters of self-confidence, self-esteem, and independence. So, whereas I had always felt somewhat different, now I felt a compounded sense of not belonging. But as often happens in adolescence, in the deep throes of angst, my sixteenth year also brought me my first physical interlude.

It was summertime, and I was a counselor at a camp for mentally handicapped persons. I was the swimming coach along with a fellow named Ross. Ross and I enjoyed one another from the beginning and became great friends. As the weeks passed, I was surprised, a bit unnerved, and pleased that we became lovers. Because I hadn't had a boyfriend or sex before, it didn't occur to me that I wasn't really very turned on or that my feelings for Ross were still those of friendship rather than love. What was more important to me was that finally I belonged; I conformed to the standard, and the fact that I still felt *different* didn't bother me too much. Our affair lasted the summer and when he had to return to college and I to high school, I was happy to *belong* to the society of my peers. Never mind that I still had crushes on women and that boys didn't gravitate to me except as pals; I had had a boyfriend and I was doing what was expected.

In autumn, I met Sue and couldn't stop thinking about her. She and I were in the theater club together and won parts in the same play. We rehearsed, took long walks, cut classes, and spent weekend days together. None too gradually, I recognized the eroticism of my feelings for her and then one day, while walking in the park, we kissed. I was absolutely amazed because with Ross I had never felt the kinds of rapture and pleasure I discovered with Sue. Kissing led to hugging, hugging led to touching, and touching led to my first lesbian experience. I was happier than I had ever been in my life but couldn't understand why with Sue I didn't feel *different*, even if loving her made me realize that I didn't *belong* to the same lifestyle as that of my friends. Trying to find the right balance, for the next few years I had a boyfriend and a girlfriend. I had affairs with men, relationships even, but I felt most connected and right when I was loving women. I knew that I could wholly disclose myself to women in a way I could never reveal myself to men and in doing so, I would feel a oneness with—not a difference from—another. A confusion arose, however, because I was still unable to let go of external pressures and embrace being gay, resulting in a paradoxical situation of learning to feel akin with a lover and yet still feeling that I did not belong to the society as a whole.

Moreover, this ambiguity created a number of other problems. First of all, regardless of reasons for being so, a closeted life is a terrible and damaging thing. My self-esteem eroded, self-worth deteriorated, and anxiety and confusion ruled. Second, my issues of *difference* and *belonging* did not disappear but rather intensified and led to an inability to truly connect, a sense of estrangement, and even low-grade depression. Third, because I lacked self-acceptance, I couldn't grasp the key to belonging, regardless of appearances; in the end, all I belonged to were appearances.

I am in my early forties now and have been out for more than half my life. There have been the usual obstacles, of course, associated with being a lesbian, such as the straight world's overt and covert discrimination, unwarranted hatred, unjustified assumptions about who or what I am, and attempted marginalization. Those same obstacles have, it's important to note, led me to become more aware of and involved in politics, both sexual and conventional, to realize a more tolerant view, to act out of compassion and sensitivity rather than fear, and finally, to assume a certain confidence in my choices and their consequences.

The *difference* and *belonging* thing was only confusing and complicated to me when I was unprepared to accept the inner call of recognition. We are each unique but not different. We are struggling to find a place for ourselves, but the notion of belonging rests in knowing ourselves. Being gay is not an entity that separates us but rather joins us to something extraordinary and fine, allowing us self-expression, identity, and completeness. When we belong to ourselves, to each other, we sit close to the warm, glowing hearth of human love and experience.

Chapter Nine

Be True to Yourself

By Edward Conlon
(Queen Eddie)

If this book is published as planned and fate has chosen to keep me in this world, I will have celebrated my sixty-ninth birthday by its publication—an auspicious age for a gay man, don't you think? Also, I will have shared thirty-eight years of love with my life-partner, Shawne. If only for this reason, I give thanks for a wonderful life. There is, however, so much more I would like to tell you. Although I have spoken at colleges and to various organizations, I am especially grateful to have this opportunity to visit with you, our younger generation, through this book.

From my very earliest childhood recollections (back to age three), I have been gay. Through my teens and into maturity, I never questioned my sexuality. To me, the attraction to my own sex was quite natural and at no time was I curious to explore an opposite-sex partner. I was able to accept the normalcy of being homosexual without repression, confusion, or guilt. I realize that there are those who struggle with sexual identity, those who live with self-imposed guilt and shame. Should this be your case, I urge you to untie those mental knots. Accept the "I am, that I am, what I am" philosophy, and be true and proud of yourself. If you need to confide in or seek professional help and you live in or near a city that has a lesbian and gay center, contact them. In all probability, you'll find a Gay Youth Alliance or some other youth-oriented group under its umbrella, where you'll be able to meet and discuss questions in a safe environment with your peers.

Coming out to yourself is a first step on the ladder of acceptance and happiness. One of the most important acts you can commit is to come out to everyone who loves you. But the timing of this must be when *you* think it is appropriate and, just as important, done with love as your motive.

Because being gay was natural and normal to me, I never flaunted it to impress anyone or to hurt them. I was a polite, well-behaved student with good grades who would have preferred home economics to wood and metal shop, classes for which I had no talent. I refused to play football, baseball, and basketball, and, with special dispensation, was excused from physical-education classes. So much for compulsory macho training! However, when I enlisted in the United States Navy, I excelled in physical boot-camp drills, much to my own surprise and the envy of some others. This experience proved I could do as well as, if not better than, any man. And this is true of all gay men.

Aside from testing my abilities, the military also introduced me to the first true love I was to know. From the moment he smiled and our eyes met, I felt a flow of energy through my body that I had never before experienced. With open hearts, we became intimate and shared our liberties together. Fifty years later, I love him no less. We have kept in touch. He married and is a good husband, and proud father and grandfather.

My "finishing school" after the military was Greenwich Village in New York City, where I began to lay the foundation of my life as a gay man. I lived there in the dark ages of the '40s and '50s when homosexuality was but a whisper of gossip and, during that time, saw an undercurrent of restlessness and change gradually begin to take hold of society. Hare Krishna, flower children, beatniks, hippies, underground dance bars and private clubs, go-go boys, Korea, Vietnam, and leather and biker bars seemed to fuse like patterns formed in a kaleidoscope. In the gay community, this restlessness climaxed in the Stonewall Tavern Rebellion, which was the "outing" of today's gay, lesbian, and bisexual movement. Surprisingly, the rebellion wasn't executed by the long-repressed older generation, but by the frustrated anger of youth—youth who no longer felt shame or inferiority because they were gay. And they inextricably changed our world. Following the example of their young cohorts, elders picked up the cause and began to lay the social and political foundations we now enjoy.

Some people would have you believe that gay relationships don't last, but it was during my New York years that I met my life-partner, Shawne, at age thirty-one. We enjoyed the excitement and glamour that New York City had to offer and moved on to Erie, Pennsylvania, where we owned a small business for five years. After our families died, we headed west to San Diego, where we still reside. It has been thirty-eight years now, and you might ask, "What is the secret of a gay marriage?" There is no secret beyond being each other's best friend, respecting each other with politeness and concern, and loving—loving that is rekindled daily. Except that my spouse and I are of the same gender, our marriage is no different from any other, gay or straight, that is childless. Well, in truth, there is one difference: In our marriage, one of us is Queen. Let me explain. Through one of life's follies and caprices that led me to these pages, I donned drag for the first time at age fifty-four and entered a local drag contest on a whim. To my surprise, I was crowned queen! What was to have been a camp title lasting only one year has endured for fifteen. I kept my name so as not to lose my identity, thus the persona of Queen Eddie was born and has created a sometimes hectic threesome in our relationship. The title led to an invitation to write an advice column in a local gay publication, and its success opened doors to a world I couldn't have imagined as a youth. The *San Diego Union*, our city's mainstream newspaper, not only did a lengthy interview, but also printed my picture in drag on the front page of its local news section. The caption read: "Make Way Dear Abby, Move Over Ann Landers, Queen Eddie is Hot on Your Heels with Some of the Best and Sassiest Advice in Town." This was followed by a television interview that received positive feedback and, suddenly, I was out to friends, coworkers, neighbors, and an entire city. Since then, I've been at City Hall with two mayors, on the arm of congressmen, chiefs of police, city councilmembers, and Hollywood celebrities. I've received plaques and awards, and have twice had days proclaimed "Queen Eddie Day" by San Diego's mayor. Through it all, Shawne has kept his sense of humor, and our marriage has not only worked, but thrived. And these have been the most productive and rewarding years of my life.

The youth of today are the world's future. Without you, we cannot move forward. Morris Kight, a senior gay activist, once said, "Not today, not tomorrow. But eventually this country will treat gays with the disinterest they deserve." Get involved in your community; become active in its workings. Volunteer a few hours of your time to an organization of your choice. Be aware of the politics that surround you; register when you can and take an active part in the voting process. It is better that you help shape the laws by which you live than to live according to dictates thrust upon you by others. Through your efforts, Morris Kight's words may one day ring true.

You have but one great enemy, and that is ignorance. Educate yourself so that you can educate others. Become a doctor, butcher, member of Congress, trucker, mayor, actor, designer, law or military officer, or—yes—a drag queen. But whatever you do, do it well, do it with pride and dignity, and do it for the next generation of young people.

Chapter Ten

Elemental Wanderer

By S. E. Gilman

A message in a bottle. This is a message to whoever reads this, whoever needs this. This is a message floating on the sea of random currents of words and space, of history and intentions, hoping to find its home. This message surfaced from my internal sea of self which has wandered from shore to shore. Perhaps there is a young woman or man of a new generation who may pick up this bottle in the world of the late '90s, and maybe in 2001, a young woman or man who will be inhabiting a world different from my own, both for good and ill.

What can I tell you about a past of mine so recent and brief, which may seem foreign to you? For me, at forty-something, this past is really just yesterday. What can I say that may outlast the brush of time accelerating, rushing past us?

Time strips us down. Thoreau said "simplify," and I know a man beloved of life and a friend full of laughter, who exemplified that word of wisdom. He wanted to live so much longer than the time he was given by the AIDS. He said that finding spirit, finding peace and appreciating the beauty of every human and earthly moment, reconciled his wasting away. "I'm satisfied. Maybe it took this illness," he mused on the phone. Then he laughed. "I have all the time in the world now, each and every day. It's like being rich and not having any money." He died, but he was worn true.

But this is not the same truth for everyone. Death did not make life precious for the first woman I loved, the woman I came out with and who changed my life and ended her own. She was twenty-one. She chose death because to live the struggle to make sense of things, to make a living, to heal and make herself whole was overwhelming. Before I met her she had been raped and had to defend her virtue in a court of law where she was treated as a sluttish target, and not as a victim of a violent crime. She lost her straight friends by becoming my lover. She was broke, disillusioned with school, flunking out. By her own choice, she took a pawnshop gun out to the countryside, and she chose a bullet to stop the confusion of living. We loved, we fought, we came out together on hostile ground, and I wanted her love and I lost her. Inside her pain, oblivion would be release; she chose death because every earthly, human moment was squeezing life from her.

Loss after loss, meaningful and meaningless, we go on. Surviving is lonely, terrible, ordinary human suffering. It is something we share with opened eyes, with an opened, sometimes violently opened, compassionate heart.

Here are things that last: the knowledge of yourself and your path growing within. They are elemental, and elements cannot be reduced. They stand unto themselves, and they work together and create a world. The ancient Greeks spoke of four elements they could see and touch. All native people know them: air, earth, fire, water.

AIR

Struggle is a dance in the air, sometimes with the wind and sometimes against it, sometimes with death or danger itself, and sometimes only with wounding shame. The struggle of air is in-your-face. It may take the dramatic form of a catcall or, worse, of a basher, or a simple, sudden acknowledgment of the effort it takes just to be who you are and stay alive. And yes, struggle will wear you down, but it may also wear you true. Don't be afraid; the wind always wins in the end when it robs us of breath, when our little wind is given up to the bigger one we dance with. Is the dance precious to you? Can you choose to be who you are, to love the dance of it even as it takes so much energy, so many losses, so many years? We breathe, we open, exhale, go on, go on.

EARTH

If the struggle of wind is allowed to do its work, you will be building up, eroding down. The wind that wears you true is the miracle of the mountain. You are creating internal terrain, twining paths of rivers, valleys through steep badlands, natural bridges that will link you to others. Wearing true is earth, digging into earth; stone, metal or gem, you will find inside a core integrity. That core may try to save you no matter how much you may want to cease the struggle and give in to self-destruction: too much risk, too much drugging, too much drinking, abusive lovers, bad choices. Like falling, like descent, you may hit bottom after bottom. But down deep is the jewel-self, the core love of the dance that may help you choose life again. "Give chance a chance," wrote a poet-friend when my lover died. Stripped down, what is important, what is left to us? To love, to let go, to give, to know what we really need.

Please don't mistake the core of integrity for the ego, the little self. Don't even mistake it for your gay, or lesbian, or any gender identity. Your gay identity is an adjective, not a thing, not a noun. Your whole self is larger than all the labels put together. The earth in you is the solid ground of human be-ing, and it too shifts, metamorphoses. But even as the self-shape shifts, knowing grows deep. Conflicts can be good. They cause us to dig for our truth. How else to unearth dirt from buried treasure?

FIRE

Light to see by, to light our way. Love is burning, clinging, transforming fire. Love with sex, or love without sex, love of knowledge about who we are and from where we've come, and where we want to go, love of getting there with one lifelong companion or many companions who travel this road with us. We are not alone. Each of us carries a spark of the whole, each of us a divinity whose dark and light combined make our mortal flame flicker and glow with the light of attraction, the heat of desire to join with the light and dark of our sister, our brother, our beloved.

Passion is spirit embodied. The world, ruled by the deliberately ignorant, the greedy, violent, or misled, mistakes our love for their own embodied spirit disowned; it has made lesbian, gay, bisexual, and transgender people carry the shadow-sex of the straight-and-narrow—their guilty pleasure, their fantasy desire and disgust, their relief in scapegoating so they can avoid feeling, avoid knowing, avoid understanding themselves. It has been the same for people of color who have carried the burden of "animal," "savage," and "violent."

Still, we burn. We burned quite literally—witches and faggots—during the end of indigenous nature religion and at the dawn of the domination of Judeo-Christian orthodoxy. Figuratively we always burned and shed our light by practicing every art, every skillful means known to humankind: music, painting, dance, design, theater, cuisine, debate, statecraft, warcraft, healing, writing, philosophy, religious life, learning, invention. The story of culture *is* the story of lesbian and gay fire—a love for life, a passion for creation, for meaningful work, for beauty. It is our very gift of light that sometimes burns our fingers, blinds us.

Many of us have tried hiding that light for our safety. To acknowledge that passion for life, that love of ourselves and for our own kind often meant beatings, family abandonment, social ostracism, arrest, financial hardship, "treatments," or "cures." For some, the closet was not merely a convenient option, it may have been the only safety. Some need that safety still. Like choosing between half-life or half-death, the closet provides protection even when it suffocates the flame. Sometimes this asphyxiation has produced astounding degrees of self-hate. What could be more toxic, more self-consuming than both noble and carnal love, our embodied spirit, turned inside and hidden? This self-hate, closet hidden, then can be calculated and projected out to sabotage those who would blow its cover, creating Roy Cohns and J. Edgar Hoovers.

Still, some of our family accomplish great things in hiding. They may think of themselves as realists, intensely burning their penlight on a single spot, surrounded by constant threat of public ruin should their love call down scrutiny. I hope those public figures who do have something to lose may someday choose to risk losing their cover to regain their honesty. A realist, too, needs air and light, needs to touch that burning core integrity. Like active dreaming, reality can also be created to have a different outcome when a risk is taken, and by that action, the rule of silence and darkness can be changed.

Fire creates, fire destroys. Because of the social movements of the '60s and '70s, because of centuries of abuses against African-American civil rights, because of an awful war in Southeast Asia, out of pain and tragedy for many peoples, the gay and lesbian movement was born at Stonewall, and the first wave of lesbians and gay men had the lucky luxury of casting off fear for our physical or psychic safety in public, outing ourselves, and letting the light fall where it may. In doing so, we shine brighter. If you're out, thank yourself. Coming out takes great and ordinary courage. Coming out for some of us had the glow of the inevitable around it; some of us can't pass. An example: I often look at the baby picture of me at four in my baseball hat—natural butch. I couldn't hide myself if I tried, and I don't want to. Come out. Let your love burn to that core. Let your light shine for the cautious, the undecided. They are watching for you.

WATER

There is a flow, political and personal, of confluence, willingness, and time. Time has a flow, and the heart ebbs and floods. I don't know where these rivers converge into the sea, but water, flow and the wind dance are much alike. Although the struggling wind can be sudden and brutish, then disappear as quickly as it stormed, trial by water may prove gentler but more relentless. When you've given your best and your best is swallowed up, or when you're dog-paddling, treading water, advises the I Ching, act like water. Water fills up the depths; it gets skinny, it grows wide, it trickles, and it floods. It releases pressure when it must, seeks and sinks to its natural level—adaptable, changeable in state, part of a cycle of fullness and drought.

In terms of the tide of time and in terms of politics, you and I (and whoever else is reading this book) are an essential wellspring of a social and civil rights movement. The flow of justice appears now as isolated victories, and later as erratic mean-spirited attempts that force simple respect and common sense to evaporate into thin air. One city passes a domestic-partners ordinance, while another punishes a lesbian couple by breaking up their family and sending their child to a foster home. One state looks the other way when men and women are assaulted by hate bashings, while another state considers permission of lesbian or gay marriage. Granted, no tide is so schizophrenic as

82

human doings. But geologic time created the ice caps, then caused them to melt and recede. Today, many people around the globe are fighting for their right to exist. Identify yourself as lesbian, gay, bi, or transgender and seek to serve. Develop common causes whenever you can. Know that there is a tide in our affairs, and that when we stand up for others who are oppressed, we also stand up for ourselves. Expect the tide to sometimes rise, sometimes fall. Only if you are there can you quench a thirst for justice at the high watermark.

Lastly, there is ebb and flow of the heart. Like the sea, it too is a mystery. If you are searching for love, search yourself. Bide your time until you are satisfied with the ebb and flow inside your own life. See if you can keep promises to yourself; settle in for a life with the person you know the best. Just for a while, don't abandon you.

If and when you find your mate, your beloved will not be the person you expect. Gloriously imperfect, their skewed good looks will list oddly to one side of their nose, or they'll wear an ugly, ridiculous hat, or be rebounding fresh from a bad break up. They will scare you. They will be damned inconvenient. But you will find all of these traits amazingly charming and fascinating, perhaps for years, until you start arguing over the very quirks that you had found attractive but now present endless opportunities for power struggles. If there are arid spaces between you, drought may be a time for choosing separate paths. But if you know in your heart you have loved no one like you love her (or him), and you are wading knowingly into fire, this is flood water, friend.

Now is the time to jump into the deep and flow, with a bit of persistence, luck, and faith. If you have built love on a base of trust, know you can mend broken trust. If you do not lose faith in the fact that you love her and she loves you, you have a shot at surviving the rocks that would break open the fragile craft each of us learned to build from the scraps of childhood. We sail on this ocean in a canoe called "relationship" that was constructed painstakingly by every zinger your mom hit your dad with, or every time your dad hit you; built-in is every memory of punishment, every addiction or covered-up abuse, every chaotic family fight or ice-chilled silent treatment. It's one shitty canoe, judging by my own experience in my family of origin; I never knew what healthy, intimate love for a partner looked like, sounded like, acted like.

My lover and I hit some rocks five years ago. She was full of rage and terror of abuse and abandonment. I withdrew; I attacked and defended; I looked for an opportunity to bail. From breakdowns to breakthroughs, she and I made a conscious decision to rebuild instead of bail.

Get thee to a counselor, get thee working on your own crummy canoe, because canoes are fragile. It may be that we cannot love until a canoe breaks and we lose our familiar habits of defense and protection; perhaps we cannot truly love another until our hearts break open to the most familiar of wounds, wounds harboring the most familiar voices of our past, our caretakers, our judges, impossible first-family-dependent loves, unfulfilled wants, frustrations, and fears. Perhaps we are meant to break apart and be washed away before we can come up for air.

Because we were both stubborn, because we learned to appreciate the fighter in each of us, my lover and I made it through the rocks, canoe intact, and flowed on. We flowed together fourteen years. It amazes me, too.

But love cannot conquer all. There was a shock, a final rapid we could not negotiate—constant change. We abandoned the relationship to save an abiding friendship. Though the decision and loss is heart-rending hard, no love is in vain; each trial, whether success or failure, brings us closer to knowing our limits. We own the mistakes, the wrong turns. This is the advantage of age: wisdom and abiding curiosity. I still want to see how life and love come out.

ALL FOUR CORNERS OF THE WORLD

The path we're on is like no other. This is why I hope you'll leave a message too, a marker at the elemental corners of your life as you round them. For although we travel solo, we are not alone. Everyone who has come before us has laid down a road and a story—paths that crisscross the world. Many roads will be crooked, no more than trails that may go nowhere, leading to dead ends, a search out of balance—but everyone has been looking. People can tell you how they got here, where they've been, what happened and how they loved, and who and what they lost or walked away from; whether doing the things they did made a difference, or if not doing was much harder on them in the end.

They'll report the basics, just the things that matter. If they carried fire, they got burned; maybe they went down in the flood or their spring dried out. Maybe the wind scattered their earth; maybe they found dust instead of diamonds. All these things can happen and do and will—constant change, wind, and flow. But some people made choices to dance while the dust was blowing, dancing like a flame that clings to the source that feeds it—the bonds of love, right action, and searching spirit that make the dancers turn.

The Believers

Probably no area of debate has raised more hackles than the issue of Christianity vis-a-vis homosexuality. In Colorado Springs, Colorado—a town sometimes referred to as Vatican West—several dozen Christian ministries pump out antigay rhetoric and propaganda on a round-the-clock basis. Perhaps the loudest voice among them is James Dobson's Focus on the Family, which rakes in $150 million a year through radio programs and direct-mail campaigns.[1] Part of what makes Dr. Dobson's political-religious organization so financially successful has been its ability to paint homosexuality as evil. He uses the Bible as his proof.

While Dr. Dobson fills the air waves with his brand of Bible-sponsored hate, the Reverend Ted Haggard fills Colorado Springs' New Life Church with 4,500 believers. "I would say homosexual behavior is immoral," he told Bill Moyers, in a televised interview.[2] When Moyers asked Haggard what his source was, Haggard replied, "The Bible."

On the other side of the continent, Pat Robertson's *700 Club* and Christian Coalition, the latter headed by the smooth Ralph Reed, also rake in millions through televised evangelism and direct-mail solicitation. Again, part of the ploy is to give believers something to feel threatened by, some way to enter into heaven. And the donations pour in.

Time and again these technology-based evangelists with jet-set-
ting lifestyles and influence that reaches the halls and pockets of
Congress cite the story of Sodom and Gomorrah as proof that homosexuality is a sin. But is it? Many respected theologians think not.

Of Sodom and Gomorrah, Daniel Helminiak, Ph.D., points out that
the sin of Sodom was inhospitality. As proof, he cites other references
to that city. In Ezekiel 16:48-49, Sodom's guilt is said to be "pride,
surfeit of food and prosperous ease, but did not aid the poor and
needy." Wisdom 19:13 says its sin was a "bitter hatred of strangers."
Even Jesus speaks about the sin of Sodom in Matthew 10:5-15 as being inhospitality, not homosexuality—and certainly not a loving relationship between two people of the same gender.[3]

If you were raised within a faith and wish to continue that relationship, don't despair. There are other voices, voices that preach the
gospel of acceptance. You may find those voices at the Unitarian
Universalist Church, the Metropolitan Community Church, the
Ecumenical Catholic Church, among gay and lesbian support groups
such as Affirmation and Dignity, or through your own personal study
and interpretation of Scripture. Michael Shaun Hennessey, of
Evangelicals Concerned Western Region, points to two Scriptures that
changed his life. Isaiah 45:9 says, "Shall the pottery say to the pot-
ter, why have you made me like this?" The second Scripture, 1
Corinthians 15:10 says, simply, "I am what I am by the Grace of God."[4]

Chapter Eleven

Jesus Loves You, Too

By Archbishop Mark Shirilau

I greet you as a gay man who is also bishop of a Christian church. Perhaps you have heard from your church or from other Christians that homosexuality is wrong. Perhaps you have heard bad things said about Christianity by other gay people. I hope this letter helps you understand that there is no disparity between being Christian and being gay. There is no reason why gay people cannot find the true and eternal joy that Jesus wanted to bring to everyone.

When I was a teenager, I was convinced that homosexuality was immoral. Fortunately, unlike some other people, I was never told that it was a greater sin than any others, but it ranked up there with premarital heterosexual sex and was certainly something we were not supposed to do. I was convinced that God wanted me to live a celibate life and never enjoy my sexuality.

I count myself fortunate in that my parents taught me that honesty was a great virtue. They also taught me that it really didn't matter what other people, particularly other kids, thought about me or anyone else. Our self-value comes from within, not from what others say or think. For these, and probably any number of other reasons, I never felt the urge to pretend to be straight. I didn't go to the prom because I would have wanted to take the quarterback, not the prom queen. I didn't get married to a woman because I knew that would never be an honest thing for me.

But I was convinced that God wanted me to be single and nonsexual forever. The more I studied the Bible and learned about God through faith and other knowledgeable people, the more I realized that this was not really true. Love is our most beautiful gift from God. Love is the emotion that we share with

God Himself, for the Bible tells us (1 John 4:16) that God *is* Love. No matter what I had heard before, I began to realize that God never meant anyone to live without love.

I did not know why I was gay, and still don't. I'm not sure it really matters whether it's genetics or hormones or social upbringing. But I know that it is part of my life that can never be changed, and that it is a part of my life that God wants me to celebrate.

When I was about twenty-seven, I accepted the fact that my life would be more fulfilling and, thus, happier and more useful to God if I were in love with another man. After a brief period of dating, I met Jeffery in 1982, and we began living together. We were married in 1984 in a small church ceremony witnessed by our parents. Our relationship was by no means perfect and, like any other couple, we had our disagreements. Yet, bonding with another person so closely brought a great balance into both of our lives, and we became better individuals for that reason.

During that time I also acted on my call to ministry and finished seminary for the Episcopal Church. However, Jeffery and I realized there was more that we needed to do to help other gay people know that God loves them as they are. We started the Ecumenical Catholic Church in our home. By the time you read this, there will be one hundred or more ECC ministries throughout the country as a result of that. We in the ECC are dedicated to witnessing to gay people of Jesus's love, and to the larger Church of God's call for us to love everyone.

Jeffery died in 1993 of AIDS. We knew for a few years that this would happen, and I'm not really sure whether that knowledge made it easier or harder. It did give him a chance to be fully real during the last parts of his life. He had a motto by which he lived—"Life is too short." I think it is a very great motto to live by because it really applies to all of us. Jeffery died having felt total completion in his life and ready to go home to heaven. Though I miss him greatly, the events of his peaceful death, the way he uplifted others around him at the end, and his joyous funeral bring me great empowerment.

Let me say a few things about the subject of AIDS because some of you probably don't think enough about it and others probably worry about it too much. You need to know that I am HIV-negative, even after having lived with Jeffery for eleven years, sleeping with him until the day he died, having sex with him, caring for him, and being at his side as he died. I will not get AIDS because I was and am responsible and careful, but not obsessed.

People do not get AIDS because they are gay. They do not get AIDS because they are sexually active. They do not get AIDS because God is not happy with them. People get AIDS only by having HIV enter their body. The virus lives in blood and semen. It enters the body only through direct contact. The mechanics of it are really very simple.

I know some young people who think AIDS is only a disease of older men, or leather men, or promiscuous men. Some of them have it now because they foolishly believed it wouldn't happen to them. You can get it from a person you deeply love and will spend the rest of your life with just as surely as you can get it from an anonymous encounter. You are not immune because you are young or because you are in love. Even marriage does not grant immunity.

I also know some young people who are so afraid of AIDS that they repress their sexuality and refuse to enter into a relationship. That is a tragic mistake. Safety, not paranoia, is the name of the game. If celibacy is what you want, that is fine. But don't do it out of fear of AIDS. Be careful always, but don't cheat yourself of your gift of sexuality.

Life is too short to go around without someone special to care about, to love, and to have love you. After Jeffery died, I was able to find Michael, a new partner. We are now beginning our life together, and I hope it will last until we grow old together. Gay relationships can and do work. I remember growing up with the stereotype that gay relationships always fall apart. That's just not true. I've proven it wrong once, and I now am planning to prove it wrong again.

You may be wrestling with your sexuality because of religion, or vice versa. You needn't be. It is true that some people claim the Bible condemns homosexuality. But most of these people don't really understand the Bible. In the time that the Bible was written, the pagan (non-Jewish) religions often had a belief in fertility gods. The way that crops were made fruitful was to have sex with temple prostitutes who were male or female priests of the pagan gods. While the idea of making sex a part of a religion is foreign to us today, it was the norm during the time that the Bible was written and forms the basis of the Bible's condemnation of prostitution, adultery, and homosexuality. These things were seen as idolatry.

People also point to the story of Sodom and Gomorrah (Genesis 19) as proof that homosexuality is a sin. Yet, many respected theologians say that the real story of Sodom and Gomorrah is one of inhospitality, about being rude to guests. It is not about homosexuality.

In Leviticus, two single verses seem to prohibit male homosexuality, but do they really? Remember that homosexual practices were related to pagan rituals. This is why they are called an abomination, which in ancient Hebrew is associated with ritual impurity, not with same-gender love. Also, no one in modern society lives by the bulk of laws in Leviticus. Who among us would tear down our house because it had mildew? Yet, Leviticus 14 has 24 verses that tell us to do just that. Why is it that two verses are chosen for literal interpretation while dozens of others are scrapped?

In the New Testament, St. Paul uses words that some interpret to mean homosexuality. Homosexuality in ancient Greece was very prominent, and many Greek philosophers considered it a higher form of love than heterosexuality. Ancient Greek, the language in which Paul wrote, had many terms for homosexuals.

But Paul did not use those terms. Instead, he used terms that, once again, referred to the pagan temple prostitutes. There is a good case for believing that neither Paul nor the writers of the Old Testament were talking about love-based homosexuality. And for the record, Jesus never mentions the subject at all, and His silence on the topic should speak volumes to those who would condemn it.

There are many churches that will be supportive of you, the next generation of gays and lesbians. Don't feel that your sexuality and Christianity don't mesh. They can. The Ecumenical Catholic Church has parishes in many parts of the country. There is also the Metropolitan Community Church, which is a Protestant denomination that has a widespread and loving ministry. If you feel the need to nurture your spiritual side, don't be afraid to contact any of them.

Chapter Twelve

To My Kind Brothers/ Friends/Lovers of Future Generations

I love you for your youth and wisdom.
I love you for your confusion and pain.
I love you for your horniness and lust for life.
I love you for your gentleness and passion.
I love you for your creativity and sensitivity.
I love you for your desire to love and be loved.
I love you for being you and fighting to exist
    honestly.

The things we suffer, we suffer together as an international community. Our individual lives, cultures, languages, bodies, and parents may be differ-

By Ron Norman

ent on the surface, but the reality of our gay souls and hearts are all One.

God is One, whether Catholic, Mormon, Fundamentalist, Christian, Jewish, Muslim, Hindu, Rasta, Taoist, Buddhist, Animalist, Pagan, Agnostic, or Atheist. These are all the *interpretations* of nature and the mystery of life by passionate, confused, fearful, devoted, loving, meditative, philosophical men and women.

Nature is God. We are God. Sex is God. Love is God.

Brutality, injustice, poverty, torture, murder, rape, war, rejection, prejudice, and intolerance are not God. If there is Evil, these destructive forces of human psychotic fear are it. They are pure Evil.

Lust is not Evil.

Sex is not Evil.

Loving is not Evil.

Making love is not Evil.

Do not let the crazed and fearful haters convince you that what you feel is wrong, what you need is wrong, or you are wrong. They blabber insanities, pretending that they are religious, moral, and law abiding. But they are not. They are just a mob of terrified, brutal, distorted human beings with the power to hurt and destroy all that is sacred, true, good, and loving.

What is true, what is healthy, what is natural is the existence of gay, lesbian, and bisexual desires and lovemaking throughout every country, culture, race, and religion in the world. And this is so through all recorded history.

You are not a mistake.

You are not sick.

You are not crazy.

You are not immoral.

You will not grow out of it.

You are you.

Anyone who truly loves life and celebrates God and respects God's creations must accept you, understand you, and love you . . . just as you are! If your father or mother or sister or brother rejects you, hurts you, or tries to change you, it is wrong. If your religious leader calls you sinful, he or she is speaking the words of the devil, the words of fear, the words of stupidity. If your government leaders or police condemn you or try to stop you with force or invasive laws, they are no different than fascists, communists, dictators, and other killers of the human spirit. They are the perverted ones, because they pervert the life force. They pervert all that is beautiful, sensitive, creative, gentle, natural, and loving in the world. They pervert nature.

I came out to my parents when I was sixteen. They were very sad, but they did not beat me or disown me or throw me out of the house. They accepted me and never talked about my gayness again.

Every few months, they conveniently forget that I am gay and ask me if I have met any nice girls. I tell them I haven't, that I'm still with my Asian male lover. They have met him many times and like him. But they keep forgetting the unchangeable truth.

That truth is that after ten years of sex and love, I still love him. He still loves me. Sex, amazingly, is better than ever! I mean it. Something about really loving someone, accepting each other exactly the way we are—as imperfect human beings—makes love last and sex become even more fulfilling.

My lover and I know each other and trust each other. It has nothing to do with whether or not we are monogamous. It has to do with opening our hearts and emotions, about deeply caring about each other, about sharing pain and joy, frustration and loss, failure and success, and the absolute wonder of Life.

Our bodies are not gorgeous, not ugly. We are average physically, but we are beautiful human beings, so sex and love are great.

We practice safer sex. We want to live . . . and continue to love.

Please. Please. PLEASE. Believe that you are worthwhile and life is worthwhile. Being gay is not a sin, not a curse, not a perversion. It is a beautiful part of the complexity of life.

Don't look for Mr. Right. He doesn't exist. Look for Mr. Sensitive, Mr. Caring, Mr. Tender, Mr. Honest, Mr. Friend Lover.

As long as you love yourself, you will be loved. I guarantee it! Don't give up, and don't give in. Fight for your own dignity. This is all the advice I have to give. I learned it by living and making lots of stupid, painful, terrible, hurtful mistakes. This is how we grow and change and become better human beings. This is how we become real lovers able to give and receive, instead of just demanding and blaming and feeling self-pity.

Your life is not a bad soap opera. It is not a movie. It is 100 percent real. Don't throw it away for anybody!

With deep love and respect and hope for all our happier, more sexually fulfilling, more meaningful futures, I remain your mysterious unknown big brother.

Taking Action

The next generation of gays and lesbians refuses to be victims. They understand that everyone is diminished when a single person is demeaned. And so, left on their own, they are taking matters into their own hands. They are forming Gay/Straight Alliances at high schools across the country. They are taking pride in their uniqueness, and they're setting examples for their gay and lesbian peers who can't yet come out of the closet. They are organizing politically because they understand that homophobia has no place in a democratic society.

They are reaching out to educate where the schools have failed, teaching their heterosexual peers that it is not what you are, but who you are that determines character. They are following the lead of Pedro Zamora and teaching fellow teen homosexuals to respect and protect themselves through peer AIDS counseling and education programs. They are networking via the Internet and word-of-mouth to locate colleges and universities that will provide them with a safe, supportive environment; they understand that education is the key to a better future not only for themselves, but for all of society.

And, not least of all, they are teaching pride and responsibility to an older generation of gays and lesbians, a generation that is now offering up mentors and role models so that youth will find the path a bit smoother.

Chapter Thirteen

OUT! To Change the World

In the light of my positive HIV diagnosis, it is an honor and a privilege to have this opportunity to write this essay, to attempt to reach a generation that follows me. It's impossible to know if this essay will ever go to print. But it is important to me to be able to share these thoughts with the younger generation of men and women who will follow me.

It is always difficult organizing one's thoughts, putting into words what needs to be said in a coherent and straightforward way. I've discovered over the years that my primary purpose in life must be to battle the oppression that defines these times, including the sexual oppression that is so ingrained in our cul-

By Gideon Ferebee

ture. I am certain that we are in a battle to end sexual oppression against homosexuals, children, women, and those who are less empowered. My revolutionary zeal has grown as a result of accepting that we, as homosexual men and women, are on a crusade. No prisoners will be taken. I do not always have a battle plan, but leaving my mark by trying to alter the current consciousness is never far from the front of my mind.

I live in a world that somehow rationalizes its intolerance of people with dark skin, of men and women who dare to love outside of the heterosexist norms. It holds onto religious beliefs that insist there may be only one god, one savior, one Golden Rule. Why should I, as a homosexual man, accept this state of mind that demands that we only partially love ourselves and selectively respect the other people with whom we share this planet?

This essay is crafted to inform young homosexual men and women that they should have no doubt that they have been given a gift. As homosexuals we have been granted a perspective, a way of thinking, an opportunity for being in this world that has not been given to large numbers of people. We are members of a renegade community that has not been embraced by the larger society. But spiritually our community is a powerhouse, a repository of a new consciousness. We must first be made aware that we are special and gifted. Once we believe it, the world will have no choice but to recognize it.

Our gift is not defined by the mark of homosexuality with which you will be or have been labeled. The gift you have is more akin to a responsibility to make this world a changed place. It is your responsibility and a collective responsibility to ensure that the world is not still as homophobic, not still so heterosex-

101

ist, not so consumed with racial hatred, ethnic strife, and religious bigotry when we leave this place. Whether or not we are comfortable with this mantle, we simply have no choice if we desire to be free of fear and to contribute our fullest potential to this society. We are not here solely for our personal gratification. If that were the case, we would not cause such turmoil in others.

After forty-four years, it seems rather sobering that it took me almost two-thirds of this life to better understand the nature of the gift I have been given. I have come to interpret my personal gift as a gift of expression, a passion for communion, and a love of the search for truth. I stumbled about my adolescence and much of my twenties and thirties, unsure about what homosexuality meant for me and for the dreams I have always harbored. "I wanted fame, public recognition and the instantaneous celebrity which follows pharaohs, fighters and the Chosen Few," I wrote long ago. How little did I appreciate that my gift had been given to me in order that I might achieve all of these things. However, I let the fear of exposure of the homosexual man who lived inside of me keep me silent. The fear allowed me to forgo my truest desires.

I settled for security, efficiency, and a more mundane existence.

With this essay I declare without reservation that to accept a heterosexist and homophobic status quo or to deny our personhood is unacceptable. We will never be healthy and fulfilled human beings as long as we allow others to define us, as long as we do not comprehend that this gift we have been given is bigger than its sexual manifestation. What we call homosexuality today is no more than knowing that to love another man or another woman is not about power, control, roles, or salvation. The ability to love ourselves and express this love physically is a very human expression of our potential to be complete, to be at peace with our environment. Why has it been so difficult being a homosexual in this society? Because too much of life is spent harboring doubt, wondering whether pastors, parents, and peers are right in their condemnation. THEY ARE NOT RIGHT. They are only afraid.

We cannot be happy when we feel the need to suppress a central part of our beings, when the society around us condemns our gifts out of a fear that our visions will somehow harm their tranquility. We cannot be satisfied with the status quo that allows all kinds of insidious behaviors against women, against children, and against the less empowered, and claims that homosexuals are evil and corrupt. We will not be happy or fulfilled as long as there is a doubt in our own minds that we are valuable, that we are healthy, that we are not mistakes.

Why is it that we (transgenders, bisexuals, gay men, and lesbians) are so hated and despised by the larger society? Why is the heterosexist mainstream so fearful of our gifts? We each have to answer that question for ourselves. But I am certain that the homophobia that guides this culture and has been rediscovered generation after generation is a signal we must not ignore. Our rejection is a sure sign of the power we possess, a power that is belittled and discounted constantly by the mainstream. We are ostracized to the point that we who possess this power, this gift, forget that we have it. We must work as a community to ensure that we understand that our gift is far more than a gift of sexual expression. Our gift is one of rebellion against a society that will not love us, that will not love any of its outcasts.

The resentment and anger we arouse in the mainstream is, I am convinced, a positive reinforcement, a motivator that compels us to pursue our quest for justice and equality with vigor.

Our desire for respect—and even the love that every man, woman, and child deserves—cannot be a misguided, wrongheaded objective. The dignity we reach for has to be a basic element of how this society approaches every one of its members. Ours cannot be a struggle merely for gay and lesbian rights.

When we compartmentalize our struggle by chanting slogans like "Two, four, six, eight. Gay is just as good as straight," we minimize the impact of what we are able to achieve. We are struggling for human rights, dignity, and respect simply because we deserve it as persons. Neither our sexuality, our race, our age, our sex, our religion alone is the prime characteristic of what makes a human being or why a human being should be loved and honored. When we allow one defining characteristic to limit our wholeness, when we allow others to label us and put us in boxes, we become less than who we are and our gift becomes less effective in changing the world. And, no matter how we deny it, our mission must be to change the world. If not, we may as well return to our gay and lesbian bars and dance our lives away!

One thing I have learned in life, and this I believe with my whole heart and soul, is that you cannot change anyone but yourself. Sometimes I am frustrated with the leaders of the gay and lesbian civil rights movement because their attention and focus seem to be on changing others: moving legislators to enact laws, moving clergy to rethink their biblical beliefs, moving ordinary and extraordinary men and women to abandon years of prejudice and fear. It ain't gonna happen. The only person one can change is oneself. Parents invest incredible amounts of time and energy in controlling their children. Some young rebel, some conform to the wishes and dictates of guardians. But I suggest to you that very little of this effort results in any real change in the basic human patterns that children will exhibit in their quest to become themselves.

I am suggesting that as homosexual men and women we are treated very much like children in this society. Society expends tremendous energy trying to control our behaviors. But even in the face of overwhelming hostility and violence, we make extraordinary attempts to be ourselves.

What is it to be gay, to be lesbian? Some leaders in the community would have us believe that they know or that they have completely defined what it is to be gay or lesbian. I suggest they aren't leading our quest for personhood or our community's struggle for civil rights anywhere worth going. We must be less concerned with what it is to be gay, lesbian, bisexual, or transgender, and become engrossed in what it is to be a person.

We must be about changing ourselves from mere stereotypes of gayness and lesbianism into prophets, revolutionaries, social scientists, researchers, leaders and healers, movers and shakers. Only by redefining ourselves as whole persons who are in part (just a part) homosexual, do we start to frame the debate with the mainstream in terms that make sense. We are not going to change the mainstream's distaste for us by becoming super homosexuals. I fear that in American society where heterosexist, racist, and sexist behavior is so utterly ingrained in the cultural psychology, it will be many long years before the mainstream relents from its constant attack against us.

We must be about turning our community (and ourselves) into shining examples of what we want this society to become. But we cannot do that if our only immediate objective is to be integrated into a racist, heterosexist mainstream as homosexual men and women. Integration did not work for African Americans and it cannot work for homosexuals. What we fail to accept, and it is difficult to accept, is that the mainstream is too intolerant of difference to welcome our difference with open arms. We must become the leaders in this society if we are ever going to affect how this society treats us. That is why I say we must change ourselves and become far more visionary than living out limited gay and lesbian lives. We have got to see ourselves as part of a much larger movement for social justice, equality, and respect for personhood. Otherwise, we will continue to confront a hostile culture, wondering why the mainstream society still has not opened itself to embrace us.

I definitely believe in God, a high power, a Universal Knowledge, the Force. I do not believe that I am a mistake because I have the audacity to love men, because I have the voice to proclaim that my loving another man cannot be an error. I must believe that God has sanctioned my life, my personhood, and that my socially disregarded homosexuality is not merely my personal, willful rebellion. Had that been so, I might have abandoned it long ago, if in letting go I might have realized my truest dreams.

We are not mistakes. We have a very definite mission to change ourselves and transform the world no matter how long it may take. We have been chosen and given a gift of self-realization self-actualization that so many in the mainstream deny in their effort to "fit in" and "be a part of." We also want to belong to the larger society. But we must recognize that we and that larger society are on a pilgrimage. As homosexuals, we are some of the earliest settlers during a period of incredible social transformation. We have been given a vision of what it can mean to be a whole person. Now we have to design a revolution so that we can share this vision with a frightened and traditional population who would rather not have to confront our power.

We have been deliberately burdened with a label that we must not grow to accept or to tolerate. I am more than the homosexual label that society would wrap me in and that many of our leaders would so readily embrace. I sincerely believe we have been given a gift and must use that gift to change the status quo. What other purpose would there be to have placed us in such a hostile world? What better reason for us to continue to strive to be examples of what personhood is really all about?

Chapter Fourteen

Learning from Les Ms.

By Elizabeth "Liz" Cramer

I would like to pass on to you what I learned from the group members of Les Ms., a coming-out support and educational group for women that I co-facilitated from October 1994 until June 1995.[1] During that time, ninety-four women attended the group at least once. Some of the issues raised were applicable to those who were seventeen as well as those who were forty-five. Although any issue or experience affects a person in a unique way, you may see parts of yourself in them.

I learned from Les Ms. members that coming out is a process rather than a one-time event. We are constantly coming out—to ourselves, to our friends, to our teachers, to our family members, to our neighbors. No matter how old we are, we still face decisions about coming out—when, to whom, how, why, and for what reasons. We make these disclosure decisions in the best way we know how given our circumstances. It may feel right to come out in some circumstances, while in others it may seem right to remain silent. Sometimes we may regret that we told significant persons in our lives about our sexual orientation; they may use this information to hurt us. Other times, we may get a positive and wonderful response from someone we expected to be unsupportive. No one else can make a disclosure decision for you; it is something you need to decide for yourself. You may want to think about the possible outcomes of telling others about your sexual orientation and to whom you might turn if the experience turns out to be negative.

Information about our sexual orientation may be shocking or hurtful to others. Consider their feelings. It might help to remember that others' difficulty with your sexual orientation does not mean that you are bad, wrong, abnormal, or sick. They grew up in a society that fears and does not understand persons who are not heterosexual. Someday they may understand and accept you. If they don't, it is not because you don't deserve to be understood and accepted. Find people who will understand and accept your disclosure. These peope might include a good friend, a religious leader, or someone at a support group, lesbian/gay community center, or hot line. If resources are unavailable to meet your needs, then create a group or organization. A small group of female and male young people came to the South Carolina Gay and Lesbian Community Center one day and said they wanted to start a youth group. And they did!

Support groups may help you to connect with other people who are working through some of the same issues. One member of Les Ms. talked about why she initially decided to attend the group: "I was really clear about my orientation but I wasn't real clear about what my identity was, what it meant to be a lesbian, what the culture was, what I could expect out of my life. I needed a place to be around other women just to learn and grow, a place that wasn't a bar and that wasn't an unhealthy place for me to be, a place where I could find someone with similar values and thoughts, and kind of grow up in the world."

A benefit of support groups is that they can be safe places for expressing feelings. Another member of Les Ms. made this comment about the group: "It's helping me to open up a lot more to people I most often would not open myself up to. . . . The group helps me to think better about myself after I leave."

Being lesbian, gay, bisexual, or transgendered is just one part of a person. Other parts of people may be important too, such as ethnicity, race, gender, or class background. These other characteristics influence a person's experience as a lesbian, gay, bisexual, or transgendered person. Growing up African American and lesbian is different from growing up white and bisexual. Sexual orientation may be the primary identity for one person, but race may be the primary identity for another. We can learn from each other about our uniqueness. We are the same; yet we are different. You have your own unique background that shapes who you are, your values, the way you communicate. You can share your complexity while learning about the complexity of others.

You will also learn that people come out at different times in their lives. Some women in Les Ms. knew they were lesbians at a very early age while others came out in their forties or fifties after living in a heterosexual marriage and raising children. There were women who identified as bisexual and currently were in a primary relationship with a man, and women who identified as bisexual and were in a primary relationship with a woman. A few group members identified themselves as bisexual after leaving heterosexual relationships, and then eventually decided they were lesbians.

The group taught me that it is sometimes very hard to be lesbian or bisexual when one is taught from an early age to seek the approval and love of men. I heard women tell stories of ways they were told they should dress, act, and talk in order to catch a man. I saw women struggle with whether they could still be feminine and be a lesbian while others struggled with whether they could be a woman and have masculine characteristics. Whatever their circumstances, the women tried to find a niche, a place where they fit in a world that didn't want to let them in.

Within the group, same-sex relationships exhibited the same full range of emotions as heterosexual relationships—exciting, fulfilling, intense, damaging, painful, and difficult. Few women at Les Ms. were in long-term, committed relationships and few found support for their relationships outside of their lesbian friends. Sadly, nearly half of the women in Les Ms. reported that they had no other resources or sources of support besides Les Ms. Some had experienced abuse by their heterosexual partners. Those who were just coming out felt at a loss as to how to go about meeting women and wondered about the ways lesbian relationships may operate differently than heterosexual ones. They were curious about lesbian sex and wanted answers to questions about it. Some of the younger women were in relationships with older women, and they questioned what they had to offer an older woman. I heard women ask whether their relationships were healthy or unhealthy. Some compromised their own feelings and needs for their partners. Some lost respect for themselves. Don't let your hunger for a relationship cause you to jump into an unhealthy situation. Treat your body and your emotions with care.

It was helpful for many women to talk about lesbian and gay history and culture. One of the group members said, "There's an educational aspect [about the group] that surprised [me]. . . . I'd been out so long...I didn't worry about the culture stuff. But we'll have these discussions and we learn about the history of gays and lesbians, and it's kind of like 'Wow! That's neat. I didn't know that about myself.' It's kind of a sense of wholeness and centeredness that I didn't have before." It may be reassuring for you to discover men and women like yourself who have existed in various cultures over time.

Support groups, feminist bookstores, and lesbian and gay organizations can provide you with information about community events. Don't be afraid to explore. You may need to attend several different events before finding an activity or group that feels comfortable for you. Find healthy ways of dealing with your sexuality—join a group of writers or a chorus, try out for a team sport, or volunteer at an AIDS resource center. Realize that alcohol and other drugs aren't solutions, simply problems.

Know that you are not alone. In one South Carolina city, ninety-four women, ages sixteen to fifty-four, of various racial, religious, educational, and class backgrounds, attended a coming-out group to offer each other support. There are hundreds and hundreds of women in cities everywhere doing exactly the same thing. Find them, and you will find people who will believe in you, who will accept you, and who will support you.

Paths of Possibility

By Susan Rochman

We had decided to meet at the food court at the mall. We'd exchanged identifying features, but I hadn't written hers down. I didn't expect there to be many teenage girls milling about the mall on a weekday. It didn't take us long to spot one another, and we exchanged quick, excited hellos. And then, there we were. Me, a thirty-two-year-old femme lesbian who was suspicious that her appearance would not be perceived as dykey enough, and Jen, a seventeen-year-old high-school student questioning her sexuality.

A few weeks earlier a school counselor had called my office—a sexual assault center in a rural, conservative community in upstate New York—on behalf of a student she had met. She was looking for local resources for gay and lesbian youth. There was no referral that I could make. No hotline. No group. No meeting place. No gay or lesbian organization. No newsletter. No bookstore. Nothing. Forty minutes east was Syracuse; fifty minutes south was Ithaca, where I live. Both of these cities have active gay and lesbian communities. But they had nothing to offer a rural teenager without transportation or parental support. So, very aware of what I was doing, I had offered myself.

If Jen had been looking for someone who could tutor her in, say, science or math, or talk to her about summer employment, local religious organizations, or virtually anything else, our meeting would not have had to take place at the mall on her lunch break from work. She could have told her parents; she could have told her friends. Instead, while eating pizza at the food court Jen and I talked—with an eye out for any acquaintances who might be near—about how it feels, and what it means, to be gay.

In large cities and in small progressive communities, there are more gay and lesbian groups and organizations than ever before. But in a rural, conservative city like the one where I worked and Jen lived, to be an out adult, let alone an out teenager is a risky undertaking. And with the rise of the religious right and recent attempts to legislate discrimination against gay men and lesbians, it sometimes feels more scary than ever.

As Jen and I established a friendship, I would be listening to her talk and sometimes wish that when I was seventeen I had known that I was gay and that my adolescent unhappiness was about more than not belonging to high-school cliques, feeling socially inept, and not understanding why it was uncool to be smart. But memories of the social reality of high school curbed this envy in a flash. The last thing people need in an environment where it is mandatory to fit in is to be utterly aware of how truly different they are and their lives will be. Perhaps it is easier now, in some places, than when I was in school. Still, I can't help but believe it is easier to figure out who you are and who you love once you have moved beyond the narrow constraints of high school.

Even if I had known that I was a lesbian, the social context for that knowledge would have left me little room in which to navigate. My experience at seventeen did not include an MTV performer as out as Melissa Etheridge, pink triangle buttons, or rainbow flag bumper stickers. There was only my cousin Bobbie, who everyone in the family said, "Just never wanted to get married."

As an adult, I have always lived in cities—by luck and by choice—that have large gay and lesbian communities. And as a lesbian immersed in the lesbian community and in lesbian and gay politics, I have shaped my world to fit my desire and my beliefs, surrounding myself with lesbian and gay friends, and making the struggle for our rights an integral part of my life. It took working in a rural community and meeting Jen to gain an understanding of the deep emotional and personal implications of enforced invisibility and the bravery it takes to search out information about gay men and lesbians when the only resource is a school library's encyclopedia.

Our conversations brought me back to my college years, when I was trying to understand who I really was and with whom I wanted to be sexually and romantically involved. Meeting Jen reminded me of the first lesbians I had met in a women's studies class in college. They were the first women who encouraged me to get involved in a school organization, the campus women's center. Now, I can't recall their names. But I'll never forget their black leather jackets, their short hair, and the way they walked into our Women in Literature class hand-in-hand.

Thinking back to that time, I can still recall clearly the afternoon I found myself walking down a eucalyptus-lined campus path telling a woman in my writing group—an incredibly femme lesbian mother with long painted nails—about *The Women Who Hate Me* by the lesbian writer Dorothy Allison, a book of poems I had absorbed and that seemed as necessary to my life as air. "When did you come out?" she asked me. I blushed and stammered, "I haven't. I mean, I'm not a lesbian."

Of course, she knew better. And I? I had to admit to myself that I found her question exciting, that I liked the idea of someone thinking that I was a lesbian. Her words carved a path of possibility; they also made me aware of how scared I was that I wouldn't get this lesbian-thing right. What I wanted, I realized, was to be out already, to have gotten beyond the awkwardness of the fact that my lips had never touched another woman's. I wanted to be beyond the nebulousness of questioning: Maybe I am, but maybe I'm not, and how do you make love to another woman anyway?

I reread Dorothy Allison's words often, trying to understand what it meant that it was women "who stir my flesh to dream."[1] And yet, how did I know I was a lesbian if I hadn't ever made love to a woman, and how would I ever even get the chance to make love to a woman if I didn't just start being a lesbian? What I wanted was for someone to rescue me from my state of lesbian virginity. But I didn't know how to make that happen. Nobody that I knew dated; from my vantage point, they just seemed to slide blissfully into coupleness.

Then I met a woman who rendered me breathless, who gave me her copy of *The Coming Out Stories*, who came over to my apartment one night, sat down on my bed, looked around my room, and said, "Don't you think it means something that all the pictures that you have are of women?"[2]

Unfortunately, she was taken. But the desire I felt, the blush in my cheeks, and the way my words tangled in my throat whenever she was near made me realize that I had to get beyond my fear to learn what my life could be. I had to be just who I was, regardless of what I had not yet done. And then came that warm spring night when I found myself standing across the street from the local lesbian bar with a woman who I knew I wanted to have as much more than a friend. In that ever-so-longed-for kiss, and later that night, I learned what I needed to know.

It is only now, looking back at all that coming out confusion, that I can identify the people and places that made it possible for me to come out to myself and to then, shortly thereafter, send my father a letter with the words "I" and "lesbian" in the same sentence. I was able to come out because I had a community to come out into. I was fortunate to have selected, unknowingly, a college with a gay and lesbian campus organization in a city with gay and lesbian groups and programs and, delightfully, a women's bar.

Thanks to a phone call, Jen and I met as she was beginning to think seriously about where she would pursue her college career. Unlike me, she didn't need to rely on luck. Instead, she knew the types of questions she needed to ask when she visited potential schools, and she made a wise, informed choice; she will be spending her next two years at a junior college with a campus gay and lesbian organization in a large city with an active and organized gay and lesbian community.

It was not only Jen who benefited from our friendship. I feel fortunate that I had the opportunity to share with Jen what others taught me: There are bookstores where all that is sold are books by and about gay men and lesbians. There are gay pride marches held each year in cities throughout the world. There are college classes taught by out gay men and lesbians where students talk and read about gay and lesbian issues. There are cities that have support groups for gay, lesbian, and bisexual youth and laws that protect gay people from discrimination. Your life can be more than what you know. You don't have to settle for anything less.

I also learned a great deal about myself through my personal struggle to balance our friendship with my professional role in the community. I was concerned, for both of us, about how her parents would react to our friendship. As a writer, I could easily envision dramatic headlines in the local, conservative newspaper about lesbian recruitment of teenagers. And when I spoke with other gay and lesbian adults they shared my concerns, if not the writer's element of high drama. Parents who are anti-gay have

119

the potential to twist the most supportive of friendships into something sick and deviant. It is the ultimate baggage that being gay carries: that we are perverted child molesters who actively recruit teenagers to our ways.

There were times when, because of these concerns, I had to tell Jen that I could not drive her to gay-friendly Ithaca or to a gay youth group in Syracuse. I'm sure that other adults and other teens would make and have made different choices. But this is the balancing act we each face in a culture that has stereotyped adult gay men and lesbians and wants to ignore the reality of gay and lesbian youth.

Recently Jen sent me a short note thanking me for her graduation gift, a copy of the lesbian classic *Rubyfruit Jungle*.[3] "You have been such a great friend to me," she wrote. "You've helped instill in me such sense of pride and confidence and I'll always be proud to say that you were a great role model of mine."

The risks were well worth the gain.

Chapter Sixteen

Addressing Harassment: You've Got to Be Carefully Taught

By Steven LaVigne

For their Pulitzer Prize-winning musical, *South Pacific*, Rodgers and Hammerstein wrote a song about being carefully taught to hate and fear. As lesbians and gays, we're made to deal with this every day in the form of harassment—both verbal and physical, blatant and hidden. Personal experience has taught me that we need to recognize it and consider ways for dealing with it.

Looking back, my first inkling that I was different from other boys occurred when I was in kindergarten. We were skipping around the room, and I was behind a girl named Patty. Her ponytail was bouncing back and forth. I remember thinking that I wanted a ponytail like hers.

My father showed little interest in me, especially after my brother was born when I was in first grade. My accomplishments were rarely, if ever praised. I shied away from most "boy" games and sports because I was usually laughed at the first time I would try something. To escape that embarrassment, that harassment, I wouldn't try again. This led to my lifelong hobbies: reading, watching television, and going to the movies. (When *Sunset Blvd.* played on television for the first time, my parents told me I would love it, and, of course, I did. I was being carefully taught.)

I grew up in a small Wisconsin city in a strict Catholic family. My mother died when I was twelve, and I knew nothing about my body until junior high school. Then something happened that made me painfully aware of it. A wise-cracking kid pointed out my erections in the gym shower. Until then, I was oblivious to them. After that, however, they became another source of embarrassment and harassment. Always called names at school, the name-calling grew worse. No matter what the old adage says, sticks and stones may break your bones, but names *do* hurt you. And they hurt for a long time. Words like sissy, queer, and fag cut deep into the psyche. What was I carefully learning?

I learned to put up invisible walls to protect myself. It has taken years to knock them down, to learn how to trust, and to take pride in my achievements. I have learned to listen to my instincts as well, and not foolishly to ignore them.

The summer of 1969 was significant for several reasons. It was the first time I felt twinges of becoming an adult. I was doing summer stock with an avant-garde theater group. I went on my first vacation alone to a big city (Milwaukee). Judy Garland died, but I didn't relate her death to the Stonewall riots or gay liberation until years later. I also had sex with another male for the first time. He was someone from my class who had been sent away because his behavior was out of control, but he was home for the summer. We did it a couple of times, but our teachers and the nuns had done their job well. We were filled with a strong fear of God, Catholic guilt, and a sense of rejection for our actions. After that, I lived in fear of my sexuality. I didn't begin accepting myself completely until after college (I was twenty-six), and I didn't march in a Gay Pride Parade until 1985.

I finally took control of my life in my mid-thirties. I enrolled in graduate school and developed a career as an elementary school teacher, learning how to raise my self-esteem and become proud of who I am. I was forty before I entered into a lasting relationship. My partner is also a teacher. His area is secondary education.

A couple of years ago, he shared with me some handouts he'd gotten from a workshop in Diversity Training and Harassment. I adapted them for my students, and have tried over the past few years to teach my students carefully how to identify discrimination and to address harassment. Hopefully, in some way, I've made a difference to them, and they're learning to deal with these problems on their own.

Harassment isn't always sexual, but it's always unacceptable and inappropriate. The term "harassment" covers a broad range of actions. Put-downs, ridicule, threats, discrimination, suggestive sexual advances, rape, and violence are all forms of harassment. Many of these are against the law. Others are not. Some are obvious; others, less visible.

Because of the values our elders were raised with, we accept, often without question, the biases of our parents, the limited tolerances of our faiths, and the sometimes narrow-minded curriculum our teachers are required to cover each year. These values are as much a part of our early learning as talking, walking, or potty training. Subconsciously, they shape our attitude toward cultural and ethnic groups different from our own. Unfortunately, we're not usually taught to appreciate the diversity that makes this such a remarkable global society. These biases, opinions, and attitudes illustrate that harassment is learned behavior and it begins early in our development. If we ignore it, harassment won't go away. It will continue throughout our lives.

Consider this. Perhaps sometime in your past you remember watching television with your parents. An inappropriate remark is made when a person from a different ethnic background appears on-screen. This is name-calling and, indirectly, can be classified as harassment. It can also be harmful because of what it potentially teaches you—that name-calling is appropriate.

Silence is another thing we learn from harassment. When we hear somebody calling names or using put-downs, few of us voice our objections. To do so would subject ourselves to ridicule, and nobody wants to be ridiculed. Instead, we're being carefully taught to be silent.

Name-calling is probably the most common form of harassment. We have all engaged in it, and we often do so without thinking, expressing sexist, racist, and homophobic thoughts.

This may relieve anger, but it also gives voice to our own internalized sexism, racism, homophobia, or other biases. Checking our awareness of this is as continual a process as growing, aging, and coming out. Unfortunately, it's not as easy to overcome, because no matter how discriminated against we may be, we can always find someone or something else to put down in order to fight off our own discrimination by others.

You don't have to go looking for harassment, only to recognize it. Ever since the Clarence Thomas hearings in 1991, harassment has become a hot topic. There are items every day on the news, it's discussed on talk shows or in the newspapers. When I was researching this essay, I found several books on the subject written specifically for teenagers. Once you're attuned to it, you can identify it.

Do you ever witness harassment at school? Probably you do. Let's say, for example, that you want to express your opinion about something in class. Instead of disagreeing with the content of your opinion, someone who disagrees with your way of thinking simply dismisses it with a personal attack or put-down. This is harassment. It's compounded if you don't respond.

Recently, I was invited to a class reunion. I hauled out my senior yearbook and paged through it. I remembered once when I dealt with harassment such as I've described as I was passing in the hall to my locker. One of the minor football heroes was standing on "the wall," a place for lettermen to gather and harass people as they went past. He asked me if I was "for real." I looked at him and said, "No, I'm a figment of your imagination." This confused him, and he never said anything to me again. I handled a potential crisis with humor. But this was a singular opportunity.

What can you do when you experience or witness harassment? How can you help teach others that sexism, racism, homophobia, and harassment are oppressions that have no place in civilized society? Fight for your equal rights. In the early 1980s, we tried to have the U.S. Congress pass the Equal Rights Amendment and add it to the United States Constitution. It was voted down because, as a friend of mine, a devoted feminist, pointed out, rather than take things one step at a time, we tried for the whole package. This was a significant setback for the women's, gay, and civil rights movements. Until it becomes constitutional law, those falling into certain groups do not experience equal protection and equal access. Those groups include gays, lesbians, women, and any minority not powerful enough to voice opposition. Unless we speak up about this problem, not every citizen of this nation will have the same rights.

You, the next generation of gays and lesbians, can and will make a difference. Coming out is the first way to do this, but you should do this only when you feel comfortable enough to do so. In the meantime, you can take other actions that will send a message to those who oppress through harassment and intimidation.

If you hear a joke that's offensive in any way, let the person know that you object. Humor certainly has its place. It's a means of dealing with stress, tension, and other problems, but there is no place for offensive jokes because, invariably, they hurt someone. Let your opinion be heard.

When faced with put-downs, speak out and address them immediately. Let the offenders know their statements are inappropriate. This may get a negative response. Keep a notebook and write everything down. By documenting the situation while it's fresh in your mind, you can refer to it if you need to in the future.

If somebody makes a sexist, racist, homophobic, or harassing statement, let them know what they've done. Tell them you find it unacceptable. Behaviors will change only if people speak out.

Write letters and editorials to your student newspaper on the topic of harassment. When electing a class president, make the problem of harassment a campaign issue if it is a problem in your school. Demand that it be addressed. It's a better political move than promising more dances and louder pep rallies!

When writing research papers and speeches for class, make harassment a topic. As I mentioned earlier, there are a number of books on the subject and they can be easily adapted for any subject area.

Create a survey and tally the results to learn how people feel about this subject. If you need an example, write to the DC Rape Crisis Center, P.O. Box 21005, Washington, DC 20009, and request a "Confrontation Survey." Ask them for permission to adapt it for a school project. If possible, publish the results.

Find out if your school has a discrimination and harassment policy that includes sexual orientation. If it doesn't, ask your social studies teacher to make this a class assignment, with everyone contributing. When it's finished, ask that it be presented to the administration in a staff meeting so that it becomes an official policy. If it doesn't get passed, submit it to the school board.

For a class project, randomly videotape episodes of television sitcoms. Show several programs in five- to seven-minute segments and ask the class to identify statements of praise and disrespect, put-downs and name-calling. The results will be surprising, but this is another example of the subliminally learned behavior of harassment.

Harassment can sometimes lead to physical violence. You

don't have to tolerate this. If you are bullied, take the next step. Document the situation. Report it to those in charge, and don't let them pass it off as a petty complaint. If your school administration ignores the incident, consider contacting the superintendent's office, the teachers' union, or the American Civil Liberties Union. Sometimes you have to fight for your rights.

Often discrimination and harassment are a cover-up for that person's own insecurities. Someone once said to me, "Those who shout 'faggot' the loudest are usually the biggest closet cases around." Confronting bigots with their own bigotry is one way to end it.

I realize that I've barely scratched the surface of this crucial issue, but I hope I've given you some ideas about addressing harassment. Remember, if you can be carefully taught to hate and fear, you can be taught to respect diversity. I wish you all luck!

Chapter Seventeen

Government Service Is Open to Everyone

By Christine Kehoe

For those of you considering a career in government service, and in particular those ambitious souls interested in seeking elective office, I have encouraging news for you: The time has never been better for openly gay and lesbian political candidates.

As we sit perched on the edge of a new millennium, we are witnessing unprecedented gains by gay and lesbian candidates in local, state, and federal elections. One of the best trends coming out of these elections is the absence of sexual orientation as an issue in the campaigns leading up to election day. Lately, it seems, it just doesn't matter whether you're gay or lesbian, but rather whether you're qualified to hold the office you're seeking—as it should be.

I know that depending on where you live, or where you are in terms of coming out to yourself, your family, and your friends, the thought of running as an openly gay man or lesbian might seem out of the question. I would like to tell you that you're not alone in that respect. If you would have told me thirty years ago when I was entering high school that I would be the first openly gay or lesbian elected official in San Diego County history, I would have laughed at the suggestion. However, back then, there were two good reasons for me to feel this way. First, the climate of the early '60s was such that coming out to myself, let alone to my family, was not an option. Second, there were no gay or lesbian elected officials for me to emulate—no political role models, if you will. Thankfully, in many parts of our country, being gay or lesbian doesn't come with the same stigma attached to it as it did as recently as ten years ago. Gay and lesbian youth are now encouraged to come out of the closet, and often entire support networks are set up to help you. Today, we find openly gay and lesbian role models in all walks of life, including high-profile personalities in the arts, sports, and politics. This combination—a better climate in which to come out and role models to pattern your lives after—speaks volumes about the opportunities that await you as you enter your teens and twenties. As you begin to formulate your long-term goals, you'll find that it's no longer a pipe dream to believe that you will one day sit on your hometown city council, run for state office, or enter the hallowed halls of the U.S. Congress. Gay men and lesbians no longer have to hide in the closet. Today, they serve their communities openly and proudly as elected officials.

I know that many of you have grown up in environments that are hostile and unaccepting, and you may be wondering what sort of life awaits you as you grow older and begin to identify yourself as an openly gay man or lesbian. You may be questioning if you'll find happiness and fulfillment in your personal, professional, and social life. You may even have the impression that gay men and lesbians are doomed to lead unhappy lives—because that's all you've ever seen or heard. My answer to you is that your life can be just as well-adjusted and fulfilling as any other person's, gay or non-gay. If you maintain your self-respect and know that who you are—and all that makes up who you are—has value, you'll be just fine. Know, too, that your physical attractions are genuine and wonderful, not imagined and depraved, as some would have you believe. Being gay or lesbian is a positive, respectable way to live. It is an integral part of who you are; celebrate it and cherish the unique qualities that make you the wonderful person you are. So don't mope around feeling sorry for yourself. Most gay men and lesbians I know are happy, vibrant people who get from and give to life more than the average person. One thing I can say about gay men and lesbians without reservation is that they know how to have a good time, so don't fret it. You will too!

One of the best things about the changing, more progressive climate in which we currently find ourselves is the opportunity we have to make a difference in other people's lives as elected officials. When I think back to my childhood, I remember sitting around the dinner table with my mom and dad and my brothers and sisters. We would often talk politics and current affairs, and I recall that many of the conversations were geared toward examining the role of government and how it should be used to help those who can't or haven't been allowed to help themselves. My folks were devoted Roosevelt Democrats—in fact, my mother worked at the Albany State House during the time when they were constructing wheelchair-access ramps for then-Governor Franklin Roosevelt who was stricken with polio—and to this day I'm driven by this sense of public service, which my parents' beliefs instilled in me. As I sit on the San Diego City Council as an openly lesbian councilmember, serving not only my gay and lesbian constituents, but all citizens of this great city, I'm humbled by the magnitude of the job. There are so many things to do, so many problems that need solving. But I'm grateful that I've been given the chance to give back to my community a slice of all that it has given to me. And I'm thankful that you, the next generation of leaders, will also be given the chance to serve your community. There is so much that you can bring to public service, especially your understanding and appreciation of diversity and your sensitivity to what it means to feel disenfranchised.

So, go out there and be active. I encourage you to get involved in your community. Work on a campaign. Enroll in a job corps program. Volunteer your time with a local charity. Experience life by taking an active role in the betterment of your neighborhood, city, state, or country. And when the time is right for each of you personally, be open and be proud of who you are. Then, take the plunge and run for office. Your community needs good leaders, and the gay and lesbian youth of tomorrow anxiously await a new set of role models. I can't think of anyone more fitting than you.

Resources for Youth

If you don't have a gay or lesbian adult you can speak to and, yet, feel a need to talk to someone about feelings of difference that you may be having, other resources are available to you. Most large urban areas now support some sort of gay and lesbian community center. These usually can be found in the white pages of your local phone book. If not, try contacting a local crisis line and asking if they have a phone number for the nearest center. Colleges and universities also can be good resources. Many have gay and lesbian academic unions that would be a helpful source of local information. Your school or public library may have a collection of gay and lesbian books. The resource chapter at the back of *Being Different: Lambda Youths Speak Out*, my previous book for gay and lesbian teens, lists more than two hundred agencies that will listen and offer advice.

Meanwhile, there are some other steps you could possibly take. One is to contact P-FLAG (Parents, Families, and Friends of Lesbians and Gays). Information it can provide may help you to better understand the same-sex attractions that you're having, and it can also give you some guidance and advice about coming out. P-FLAG can be reached at the address and phone number below:

P-FLAG
1101 Fourteenth Street, NW Suite 1030
Washington, DC 20005
202/638-4200

Two magazines that are aimed directly at gay and lesbian teens are *XY Magazine* and *Y.O.U.T.H.* Here's how to reach them:

XY Magazine	*Y.O.U.T.H.*
4104 24 Street, #900	PO Box 34215
San Francisco, CA 94114	Washington, DC 20043
415/255-1502	202/234-3562

Numerous church organizations help gay and lesbian individuals reconcile their sexuality with mainstream religious thinking. Whatever your denomination, there is probably a gay/lesbian group to reflect it. A few are listed below:

Affirmation (Mormon)—213/255-7251
Dignity (Catholic)—800/877-8797
Integrity (Episcopal)—201/868-2485

Additionally, you can turn to the Ecumenical Catholic Church (707/865-0119) or the Metropolitan Community Church (818/762-1133). Both churches reach out to the gay and lesbian community. Be sure to check your local phone directory under Churches to see if an affiliate church is close to you.

Finally, don't overlook the Internet. If you are connected to America Online or CompuServe, gay electronic forums provide information. But act wisely. Don't give out personal information, like your address and phone number, and if you arrange to meet anybody, do so in a public place like a mall. Just as there are weird heterosexuals, there are weird homosexuals. Those of us who contributed to this book want you to remain safe because there's a whole, exciting, promising, rewarding life ahead of you.

About the Contributors

LIZ CRAMER

Liz Cramer is an assistant professor of social work at Virginia Commonwealth University and a licensed clinical social worker. She has worked in the field of domestic violence since 1979 and presently serves on the Chesterfield County Domestic Violence Task Force, and also provides training for new volunteers at the YWCA women's advocacy program in Richmond, Virginia. Liz is currently involved with InTouch, a women's camping and event center, and has been an active participant of feminist and lesbian/gay organizations for several years. Her main areas of scholarship are domestic violence, reducing homophobia among social work professionals and students, and culturally competent service provision to the lesbian and gay population.

DAVE CLARK

Born and raised in west/central Iowa, Dave Clark is a farm boy at heart who has succumbed to gay flight to the cities. Dave comes from a long line of hardworking, down-to-earth people, where family picnics and softball games happened at every gathering. He attended a major university to, subconsciously, find self and happiness, and a way off the farm. Formally educated in architecture, engineering, counseling, and higher education, he is committed to teaching at small, private liberal arts institutions. Active in, and rejuvenated from, the queer movement through education, Dave serves as a lecturer, writer, and consultant in residence.

EDWARD CONLON

Edward Conlon is a native of Jersey City, New Jersey. The son of a barge captain, Eddie spent the first six years of his life on the water. He later trained in theater at the Abbe Theater School and pursued a career in sales. Along the way, he opened a framing shop and art gallery. Today, when he isn't busy tending to duties as Queen Eddie, he can be found collecting antiques, cooking, and simply enjoying life. Staying home and watching a movie with his life-partner Shawne is his favorite form of entertainment.

SIEGLINDE FRIEDMAN

Sieglinde Friedman is in the communications field and has worked in the area of international development for the last twenty-five years. Born in Tubingen, Germany, she has maintained a strong identification with her European beginnings and diversity in general. From developing public-service advertisements with the Peace Corp to forming her own film and public relations firm to working in her current post researching and writing on issues concerning humanitarian relief, Sieglinde has continued a strong interest in cross-cultural and foreign affairs. Her personal passions range from photography to travel to theatre.

GIDEON FEREBEE

Gideon Ferebee was born in the Bronx, New York, at the century's midpoint, a time that he remembers being more optimistic and full of so many extraordinary potentials. He has spent the last half of his life in Washington, D.C., where he has worked for the last three years at two organizations. His sense of the epidemic has taken him to emotional highs and lows. Diagnosed as HIV positive in 1989, Gideon believes that many of us will survive the AIDS pandemic and he hopes that the survivors will have a keener understanding of life as a result. His first book of essays, *Out to Lead,* was published in 1994.

S. E. GILMAN

S. E. Gilman is a native of Galveston, Texas. Her stories and poems have appeared in small presses since 1974, along with an occasional essay or article; the most recent fiction appeared in *The Americas Review, News from Nowhere,* and *modern words*. The story, "The Idle Time," was included in the anthology *Common Bonds: Stories By and About Modern*

Women (SMU Press, 1990); *Anyone Can Be a Target, Even Margaret*, her 1978 chapbook, was nominated for the Pushcart Prize in 1979; and "Private Life," published in *Stone Drum*, was nominated for the O. Henry Award in 1986. Gilman founded and edited *Hubris* literary magazine (1982-83). She is currently revising a second, and she hopes, seaworthy, novel.

CHRISTINE KEHOE

Christine Kehoe was elected to the City Council on November 2, 1993, becoming the first member of the gay and lesbian community to be elected to public office in San Diego. Ms. Kehoe has been active in San Diego politics and community affairs since 1978, when she began as a volunteer with the Center for Women's Studies and Services. In 1984, she became editor of the popular and award-winning weekly, the San Diego *Gayzette*. She served as one of the early directors of the AIDS Assistance Fund, which grew into the San Diego AIDS Foundation; and served as the executive director of the Hillcrest Business Association, where she worked for small business owners to cut red tape and improve communication with city government.

STEVEN LAVIGNE

Steven LaVigne is no stranger to the early stages of harassment. An elementary school teacher, he addresses it on a daily basis. His book, film, and theater reviews and essays have been published in *Scene Magazine*, *Lavender Lifestyles*, *Gaze*, *Gay Lesbian Community Voice*, and *Artviews/The Fan*. He was a regular contributor to KFAI-radio's "The Fresh Fruit Show" for ten years and is the recipient of a 1993 certificate from the Neighborhood and Community Press Association for his writing in the *Corcoran Neighborhood News*. Steven lives with his partner, theater director and teacher Douglas Dally, in Minneapolis.

GARY MALLON

Gary Mallon is a native New Yorker. He has a master's degree in social work from Fordham University and a doctorate in social welfare from the City University of New York at Hunter College. Currently, Dr.

Mallon is an assistant professor at Columbia University School of Social Work in New York City. He and his partner live with their family in Queens, New York.

JOHN MCFARLAND

Born and raised in Cambridge, Massachusetts, John McFarland studied at the Massachusetts Institute of Technology, Harvard University, and Johns Hopkins University. He was a Peace Corps volunteer in Bolivia and has worked as a research economist. His prize-winning *The Exploding Frog and Other Fables from Aesop* (with illustrations by James Marshall) was published in 1981 and his stories for young readers have appeared in *Cricket* and *Spider*. His writing has also appeared in many literary journals as well as in the recent anthologies *The Next Parish Over: A Collection of Irish-American Writing* (New Rivers Press) and *A Loving Testimony: Remembering Loved Ones Lost to AIDS* (Crossing Press).

CATHY MCKIM

Cathy McKim was born in Hamilton, Ontario, Canada. A Gemini and a recovering Catholic, she holds a B.F.A. in visual arts from York University (Toronto) and a diploma in theatre arts, acting, from George Brown College (Toronto). She is the Assistant Editor and Art Director of Moonlighters Publishing, Inc., which produces books for and about the acting and modeling industry. She has published several pieces in *An Actor's Guide to Agencies in Toronto*, and her first short story appears in *Countering the Myths: Lesbians Write about the Men in Their Lives* (Women's Press). Cathy is currently working on her first play, a collection of short stories, and the second edition of *How to Become an Actor . . . and Survive*. She lives in Toronto with her cat, Jamie.

RON NORMAN

Ron Norman is a published writer, poet, critic, editor, abstract artist, photographer, award-winning film director, teacher, and world traveler. Despite all this experience, he is not ancient and still vividly remembers being young, scared, and passionate. He lives in West Hollywood, California.

SUSAN ROCHMAN

Susan Rochman is a freelance writer living in upstate New York. She spent six years working in human services, most recently as the executive director of a sexual assault center. She has written for *The Advocate*, *Curve* (formerly *Deneuve*), and the *Progressive*, and her short stories have appeared in the anthologies *Loss of the Ground-Note* and *Word of Mouth*. She serves on the board of the Ithaca Lesbian, Gay, and Bisexual Task Force.

GLENDA M. RUSSELL, PH.D.

Glenda M. Russell, Ph.D., is a psychologist who lives and practices in Boulder, Colorado. She conducts research on a variety of issues, all of which bear some relationship to the interface of the person and her/his external world. She recently co-produced a video based on her research on heterosexual allies. She sings every chance she gets.

RONNI SANLO

Ronni Sanlo is the director of the Lesbian Gay Bisexual Programs Office at the University of Michigan. She earned a masters degree in mental health counseling and a doctorate of educational leadership, both from the University of North Florida in Jacksonville, Florida. Before joining the staff at the University of Michigan in 1994, Ronni, a lifelong Floridian, was the AIDS surveillance officer with the State of Florida for the Northeast Florida area from 1987 to 1994. She was also an instructor at the University of North Florida and an HIV/AIDS educator. In addition to founding or cofounding numerous lesbian and gay organizations in Florida, Ronni served as executive director and lobbyist for the Florida Task Force, Florida's lesbian and gay civil rights lobbying organization. Her hobbies include boating and golf. Ronni is the proud mother of two adult children and is the very proud grandmother of Elizabeth, to whom this work is dedicated.

ARCHBISHOP MARK SHIRILAU

Archbishop Mark Shirilau was born in Long Beach, California. His educational background is in electric power systems engineering, business administration, and religion. He and his partner Michael currently reside in the redwood forests of northern California along the Russian River.

RICHARD STRICKLAND

Richard Strickland is a socioeconomist whose work addresses issues of sustainable development, economic reform, and social change around the world. Born and raised in Roanoke, Virginia, he has since lived and worked in Europe, Africa, and North America, with ports of call scattered from Colombo, Sri Lanka, to Winnipeg, Canada. He currently directs a grants program in Washington, DC, supporting policy-oriented action research and advocacy that aims to improve the lives of women in developing countries and in transitional economies. An amateur photographer, poet, cyclist, and snorkeler, he cycled 250 miles in June 1996 as part of the Philadelphia-DC AIDS Ride, raising funds for community organizations in the District of Columbia that serve those living with HIV/AIDS.

Source Notes

INTRODUCTION

1. Alfred P. Kielwasser and Michelle A. Wolff, "Silence, Difference, and Annihilation: Understanding the Impact of Mediated Heterosexism on High School Students," *The High School Journal*, p. 69.

2. Brian McNaught, *Gay Issues in the Workplace* (New York: St. Martin's Press, 1993), pp. 14–15.

3. Michelangelo Signorile, "The Post-Stonewall Generation," *Out Magazine*, July/August 1994, p. 88.

4. Signorile, p. 93.

5. Brian McNally, "Letters," *The Advocate*, June 11, 1996, p. 8.

ALL IN THE FAMILY

1. Linnea Due, "Young and Gay," *XY Magazine*, March 1996, p. 26.

2. Liz Balmaseda, "Fond Memories Remain: Pedro Broke Mold, Dad Recalls," *PFLAGpole*, Winter 1995, p. 6.

MAJORITY RULES

1. Louis Sahagun, "Utah Board Bans All School Clubs in Anti-Gay Move," *Los Angeles Times*, February 22, 1996, p. A-12.

2. Due, p. 26.

CHAPTER 4

1. Rita Mae Brown, *Rubyfruit Jungle* (New York: Bantam Books, 1977).

CLOSETS AND OTHER DARK PLACES

1. Larry Dane Brimner, *Being Different: Lambda Youths Speak Out* (Danbury, Conn.: Franklin Watts, 1995), p. 43.

2. P. Gibson, "Gay Male and Lesbian Youth Suicide," *Report of the*

Secretary's Task Force on Youth Suicide, vol. 3, pp. 110–142 (Washington, D.C.: United States Department of Health and Human Services), p. 110; in Kielwasser, p. 59.

CHAPTER 7

1. Paul Monette, *Becoming a Man: Half a Life Story* (New York: Harcourt Brace Jovanovich, 1992), p. 4.

THE BELIEVERS

1. Skipp Porteous, "The Techno-Religious Right," *Free Inquiry,* Fall 1994.

2. Bill Moyers, "The New Holy War," *Bill Moyers' Journal* (New York: Public Affairs Television, Inc., WNET, 1993); air date: November 19, 1993.

3. Daniel A. Helminiak, Ph.D., *What the Bible Really Says About Homosexuality* (San Francisco, Calif.: Alamo Square Press, 1994), pp. 39–40.

4. Karen Ocamb, "For Christ's Sake," *Genre,* November 1994.

CHAPTER 14

1. Les Ms. was developed and implemented by Tami Eldridge, a public health educator, and Liz Cramer. The group met weekly at the Gay and Lesbian Community Center in Columbia, South Carolina. The group was diverse and included women ages sixteen to fifty-four. More than one-third of the women were from rural areas surrounding the city and about 17 percent were women of color. The women had various educational backgrounds including women in high school and women with four-year and graduate degrees. Nearly one-third were currently high-school or college students. The occupations of the women included police officer, teacher, waitress, secretary, social worker, nurse, and cook. There were mothers and co-mothers in the group who had female and male children who ranged in age from three weeks to twenty-two years.

CHAPTER 15

1. Dorothy Allison, "What Is the Dream of Flesh?" *The Women Who Hate Me* (Brooklyn, N.Y.: Long Haul Press, 1983), p. 49.

2. Julia Penelope, ed., *The Original Coming Out Stories* (Freedom, Calif.: The Crossing Press, 1989).

3. Brown.

Further Reading

NONFICTION

Bell, Ruth, et al. *Changing Bodies, Changing Lives: A Book for Teens on Sex and Relationships*. New York: Random House, 1988.

Borhek, Mary V. *Coming Out to Parents*. Cleveland, Ohio: Pilgrim Press, 1983.

Brimner, Larry Dane. *Being Different: Lambda Youths Speak Out*. Danbury, Conn.: Franklin Watts, 1995.

Cohen, Susan, and Daniel Cohen. *When Someone You Know Is Gay*. New York: M. Evans, 1980.

Marcus, Eric. *Is It a Choice?* New York: HarperCollins Publishers, 1993.

FICTION

Bauer, Marion Dane. *Am I Blue? Coming Out From the Silence*. New York: HarperCollins Publishers, 1994.

Brown, Rita Mae. *Rubyfruit Jungle*. New York: Bantam Books, 1977.

Garden, Nancy. *Annie on My Mind*. New York: Farrar, Straus, Giroux, 1982.

van Dijk, Lutz. Translated by E. Crawford. *Damned Strong Love: The Story of Willi G. and Stephan K.* New York: Holt/Edge, 1995.

Warren, Patricia Nell. *The Front Runner*. New York: Bantam Books, 1975.

_____. *Harlan's Race*. Beverly Hills, Calif.: Wildcat Press, 1994.